"Don't look now, but here comes Morgan!" Katy said suddenly.

"Do you ever stop kidding around?" I asked.

She grabbed my arm, and pointed toward the music store. Morgan Granger—*the major cutie at school*—was heading right in our direction.

"Hi, Morgan! What did you buy?" Katy asked sweetly, casually swinging her ballet bag back and forth. We both had crushes on Morgan, but Katy always pushed me to talk to him.

"I got sheet music for *Circus Town,* the new play at school," Morgan replied. "I want the lead role of the Ringmaster. You're both trying out, too, aren't you?"

Katy gave me one of her looks that said, *This is your chance, Kerri—don't blow it!* But how could I try out when I freeze with fear every time I get near a stage?

Step Monsters

Karle Dickerson

Photo by John Strange

Published by Willowisp Press, Inc.
401 E. Wilson Bridge Road, Worthington, Ohio 43085

Copyright© 1989 by Willowisp Press, Inc.

Printed in the United States of America
10 9 8 7 6 5 4 3 2 1

ISBN 0-87406-375-2

To Rick and my favorite little monsters,
Brandon and Devon

One

I slumped onto my bed in the corner of my sunny, country-style bedroom. "So what if I ruin my bridesmaid's dress?" I muttered to my fluffy, white cat, Percy, as he watched me lazily through half-closed eyes.

I put my hands over my ears to block out the sounds of the wedding preparations going on all around me. But I could hear them no matter what I tried. Even with my fingers stuck tightly in my ears, I could hear Aunt Sybil fussing in the next room over my mother, *the bride*. I could hear the *clackity-clack* of the rented chairs being set up in the living room. And someone in the kitchen was bellowing, "Oh, what a beee-yoooo-tiful wedding cake!" *Gross!*

"My life is ruined," I whispered to Percy. "And it's not fair to have a ruined life when you're only 13 and 3/4 years old."

This was the afternoon of Mom and Gary's wedding and reception. Gary, my stepdad-to-be, is nice enough, I guess. He's tall, dark-haired, and just a little bit paunchy. He always acts nice toward me whenever he comes to take my mom out for dinner or whatever. He tells me jokes, and sometimes he even offers to give me a ride on his big, red motorcycle. My mom, of course, is terrified of the thing and forbids me to get on it.

Everything seemed to be going all right, but before I knew it, Gary and my mom were making wedding plans. *Wow!* I mean, *my mom married again?*

Outwardly, I've acted like I'm happy about the wedding. What else could I do? After all, the way everybody carries on about weddings, marriage must be the greatest thing in the world. So, during the weeks before the wedding, I just smiled a lot and threw myself into my schoolwork and ballet classes. I haven't said much to anyone about how I've felt. Actually, I try not to talk much about any problems. I dance them out instead. And I'm a pretty good dancer, except that getting up on stage terrifies me. That makes Madame Maur, my ballet teacher, crazy. But that's another problem.

Lately, I've been more concerned about

Mom's getting married. After all, she and I had been a team since my dad died in a private plane crash when I was eight years old. I was the one who cheered her on when she opened her interior design studio a year after that. I still miss Dad, but Mom and I were doing fine. I just didn't see the need for a new family formula.

The wedding plans also didn't take into account that I needed time to get used to the idea of being part of a new family. The weeks had flown by, and now it was only one hour before Mom and Gary would be standing in our living room in front of a justice of the peace.

For most of that last hour, I sat on my bed, grumpily petting Percy, and trying not to think about what was to come. Just a few minutes before we had to head downstairs, Mom came into my room. She looked like a vision in a stunning tea-length, peach dress.

"You look beautiful, Mom," I said, getting up and brushing her cheek with a kiss. She smelled nice, like flowers after a rain.

"So do you, Punkin," she answered.

"I'm scared," I squeaked in a little-girl voice. I felt tears well up in my eyes.

"We're going to be all right," Mom said, giving me a squeeze.

9

Suddenly we heard the front door open, and a noisy commotion followed.

"Oh," said Mom. "That must be the boys."

"Ugh," I moaned, rubbing my eyes. She was referring to my three stepbrothers-to-be.

Mom took my hand in hers. "Remember, honey. I always told you this was going to be a package deal. And next week, when we get back from our honeymoon and the boys move in, we're all going to have to get used to some changes."

I nodded my head as I tried to imagine our quiet, cozy country house with three boys making messes and running up and down the stairs. Three gross boys who screamed and yelled and rode BMX bikes in the dirt. I just knew living with them was going to be awful!

I had met the boys before the wedding, of course. We'd had dinner together twice, and once we went to a monster movie after dinner. I didn't like the slimy creatures that crawled across the screen, and I wasn't too sure about the three creeps who sat next to me. They hogged all the popcorn and made stupid jokes throughout the entire movie. It was hard to think of them as stepbrothers. *Stepmonsters* was more like it!

Aunt Sybil poked her head into my room. "It's almost time, Anita. The guests are arriving. You shouldn't be late."

Mom winked at me. Aunt Sybil is always such a worrier.

"Come on, Kerri," Mom said with a laugh. "We'd better get out there."

"I'll be right there, Mom," I said. I looked in the mirror one last time and thought again about my new stepmonsters. Justin, the oldest and just about my age, seemed to think that he could charm me with his looks. He was always flashing smiles at me, but I wasn't charmed. Anyway, I already had my eye on a boy at school. And then there was Tim, who was 10 years old and who didn't make much of an impression on me. He was too quiet. But Blake, the six year old, was an okay kid, except for his whining.

Well, there was no more time to think about them. The wedding was starting in a few minutes. I closed the door of my room and headed downstairs.

The ceremony itself was a blur. I barely recall hearing them say, "I do," and then it was time for the reception to begin. I hung around with my best friend, Katy Provender, and her sisters. Katy and I have been friends since we were babies together in the local daycare center. She knows everything about me. She even knows about my secret crush on

Morgan Granger, *the major cutie at school.*
Today, she stayed by my side and kept
reminding me to smile.

After the reception, the newlyweds got
all ready to leave for the San Luis Obispo
Airport. They were going to go directly from
California to some place in Mexico for their
honeymoon.

"Enjoy the peace while you can," my mom
said as she kissed me good-bye. My silk dress
rustled noisily against her new crisp navy blue
suit that she had bought especially for the
honeymoon. Then she and Gary dashed
outside to the car that was waiting to whisk
them to the airport.

"What peace?" I grumbled, with my smile
still pasted to my face. I turned back to face
the party that was still going full force. I
stared pointedly at my three new stepbrothers.

Blake, the little one, was stuffing wedding
cake in his mouth. Justin and Tim were in the
corner drinking carbonated punch and having a belching contest. *Can you imagine anything more disgusting?*

"Let's move to the other side of the room,"
I said to Katy in a voice loud enough for the
belching monsters to hear. But before we
could take a step, Uncle Randolph, a crazy

relative of mine, clumped us together for some video shots. He thought he'd act like a big-time movie director.

"Hug each other, and wave for the camera," he called while the video camera caught it all on tape. Blake and Tim each put an arm around me, which made me freeze in position. Then Justin threw me a grin and made devil rabbit ears above my head. I glared at him as the camera caught everything. "Isn't this a cozy little family?" beamed Uncle Randolph.

"Can you believe this?" I shrieked to Katy, who was standing nearby and watching in amusement. She kept giving Justin these looks—of disgust I hoped. As soon as Uncle Randolph yelled "cut!" Katy and I moved to the far end of the living room. We wanted to get as far away from the stepmonsters as we could get.

Katy couldn't stop laughing. She always laughs at everything. She's different from me, but we're still best friends. She and I both are in the eighth grade at San Martin Junior High, and we both take ballet class at Madame Maur's. Madame Maur adores Katy. Katy has been in lots of dance recitals, but I haven't been in one since second grade. That's when I threw up all over my Sugarplum Fairy costume right before my stage debut in

The Nutcracker Suite. I was that nervous.

"Stop laughing," I said frowning at Katy. "It's not funny."

"I can't help it," said Katy, trying to bite her cheeks. "I mean, it's just too funny to picture you living in the same house with a family of burping boys."

"It's not funny," I repeated. "It'll be torture."

"It will be torture," Katy agreed. "But look at it this way—everyone will know that you're not related by blood. You don't really look like a family. I mean, your hair is dark brown, and the boys all have that dirty blond hair. Your eyes are green, and theirs are blue."

That's just like Katy to notice things like that. Of the two of us, she's the more outspoken. I'm not shy exactly. I'm reserved, as Mom calls it.

The party finally ended. Some relative of the stepmonsters rounded up all of them to go back to his family's home for the week. I smiled—a real smile this time—as I watched them go.

"See you next week!" Blake called out to me as they left.

After everyone had gone, Katy and I went up to my room, and giggled and gossiped about stuff that was going on at school. Katy did funny imitations of my stepmonsters that had us cracking up for hours.

Then Katy left, and I had to think of something to do next. Unfortunately, the next thing was trying to be nice to Aunt Sybil, who was staying with me for the next week.

"I don't think I can stand it. Aunt Sybil will drive us both bonkers. I just know it," I said to Percy. He had landed with a soft plop on my lap. He leaned his cheek into my hand so I would scratch him. He immediately started purring like crazy.

"Traitor," I said affectionately. "How can you purr at a time like this?"

Percy yawned and stretched, but he didn't answer my question. "You might as well know," I went on. "Your life is going to be turned upside down, too. I hate to tell you this, but Gary's kids have a dog! And he's not a little dog. He'll be coming here to live with us next week." I said the word *dog* in a creepy voice, but Percy didn't seem to care. He simply curled up for a snooze and continued purring contentedly.

I sat for a few moments and tried to get motivated to change into jeans and to start cleaning up the mess. At least Mom had arranged for a professional cleaner to come in and do the worst parts. And the rental guys would come to take back the three white tables and matching chairs that were cluttering our living room.

I sighed. If only Aunt Sybil weren't here. The last thing I needed was to have her around. She isn't mean, but she isn't very nice, either. The biggest problem is her allergy to cats. I think she also may be allergic to kids, especially to me! Whenever I come into a room where she is, she always seems to sneeze.

"There you are, Kerri, dear," Aunt Sybil said, walking into my room. Just looking at her can give me the willies. She always has granny glasses resting on the end of her nose, and her short hair looks just like a skunk. Parts of her hair are black, and other parts have strange blond streaks. When she walked into my room, she was carrying a can of disinfectant spray. "We'd better get started on this mess. When is that cleaning lady supposed to come? And, Kerri, toss that cat outside."

She sneezed, of course, which made Percy sink his claws into me.

Then she sprayed a disinfectant cloud around me, which made Percy sink his claws into me even more.

"Ouch!" I yelled.

"I'm keeping that cat's germs from spreading," Aunt Sybil said with a sniff. "Now toss him out!"

I guess Aunt Sybil probably wished that she had a can of something that would do the same to me. Sometimes I can't believe she and Mom are sisters. They are so different. She gave one last spray and walked downstairs, still spraying all the way.

"I don't think I can stand this," I wailed miserably to Percy, as I took him to the garage and made a bed for him. Percy isn't really an outdoorsy cat.

Suddenly, the doorbell rang. "Kerri, will you get that?" Aunt Sybil's voice echoed from the living room, where most of the reception mess still sat. It was obvious that she didn't want to be interrupted during her germ-finding mission.

"Yes," I mumbled. It was probably just the guys coming to retrieve their furniture.

But before I reached the door, I heard a resounding *woof* sound. It surely couldn't be the people for the tables and chairs. Cautiously, I pulled open the door and came face to face with a very large, very muscular gray dog at the end of a red leash. The dog barked loudly again as he stared at me. On the other end of the leash was Justin, the oldest of my now stepmonsters.

Only a few hours ago, he'd been in our living room, dressed in gray pants and a jacket. Now he wore an electric yellow T-shirt that had Supercross Nationals written on the front and a pair of dirty blue jeans.

"What are you doing here?" I asked. I stepped back so I wouldn't get dirt on my dress. I tried to close the door a little more so that Percy, who had followed me to the door, wouldn't flip out at the sight of a dog.

"Don't worry about Digger," Justin said. "He won't bite you."

"I'm not afraid of your dog," I said stiffly. "But you still haven't answered my question."

"Look, I've got to run. We're all staying with Uncle Paul out in the desert. We're going to tear up the trails on our bikes. It was a last-minute deal, and there's nowhere for Digger to stay. He was supposed to move in here with us next week, anyway. Tim and I thought that Digger could stay with you here this week, too. Then you can get to know him better." Justin smiled lopsidedly and looked at me like I had been waiting for this moment all my life.

"What a dumb idea," I stated flatly, eyeing Digger who looked pleadingly at me. Then the dog started licking the door. "Gross! Make him stop that. Make him go away."

Justin looked at me pleadingly. "Look, Kerri. Everybody's in the car waiting to go."

He pointed to the shiny, green and white van behind him. It was packed with kids, dirt bikes, and suitcases.

"We're all ready to go. You've just got to keep Digger. I've got his bowl, his food, and everything right here. Kerri, we're family now, aren't we? Please?"

Don't ask me why I said yes. I don't like dogs, and I don't like last-minute plans. As I slammed the door and had Digger on the leash inside my house, I made up my mind that I definitely didn't like Justin or his dumb brother with the bright ideas.

"Who was it, dear?" called down Aunt Sybil. I was peering through the front miniblinds at the van that had brought the stepmonsters to my doorstep. As the van pulled away in a puff of bluish smoke and dust, I turned back to look at Digger and his assorted cans of dog food that were stacked neatly beside his dog dishes. Percy, of course, was nowhere to be seen.

Oh, boy, I was in for it now.

Two

"KATY, it's worse than you could imagine," I wailed on the phone that night. "Justin brought his dog over here. I'm supposed to watch him for a week. And you know what the first thing he did was? He chased away the cleaning lady who was supposed to clean up the reception mess. I tried to catch them, but they took off. So, guess who got stuck cleaning the house?"

I thought Katy would be as I disgusted as I was. I couldn't believe my ears when she started to laugh.

"You know, Kerri," Katy said. "Taking care of a dog for a few days is not so bad. Anyway, you've got to admit that Justin is— well—he's not bad to look at."

"What?" I sputtered. I mean, one of the reasons Katy and I were friends is because we both had the same taste in guys. For

21

example, even though I was the one with a world-class crush on Morgan Granger, we both agreed that he was the cutest guy in school.

"Well, Justin is cute. Even you have to admit it. While you were getting more cake for your uncle, Justin got me some punch. And after we drank it, I think he was going to ask me to dance except your uncle decided to videotape your family right then," Katy said.

"Are you crazy?" I gasped into the phone. "You think Justin is cute?"

"He is," Katy said in a matter-of-fact voice. Then she said something totally unbelievable. "I'll make you a deal. Let me walk his dog, and I'll help you with your English homework all week."

"I don't need help with my English homework," I lied. "But you're welcome to walk the dog all you want. I think he's a big, slobbering mess."

"But he is Justin's dog," Katy said. "I'll have Mom drop me off at your house tomorrow after dance class, and I'll walk him."

"You're nuts," I said to Katy.

After Katy and I hung up, I was still shaking my head in disbelief. Justin was a lot of things, but I didn't think he was cute. He was certainly nowhere near as cute as Morgan Granger.

As I changed into my nightgown, I replayed the worst scenes from today's filming of *The Ruins of My Life* by Kerri Rutherford. Then I finally fell asleep.

The next afternoon after ballet, Katy and I were waiting outside of Madame Maur's studio for Katy's mom to pick us up. We both were wearing pink sweats over our leotards, and we both had messy hair.

"Don't look now, but here comes Morgan," Katy said suddenly.

"Do you ever stop kidding around?" I asked irritably.

Katy grabbed my arm and squealed, "I'm not kidding. He just walked out of the music store. He's heading straight toward us."

"Oh, I look awful!" I cried as I brushed back sweaty strands of hair from my face. Wishing that I could disappear, I backed up to the wall as far as I could go.

"Hi," Morgan said, stopping right in front of us. He was wearing a navy blue ski jacket that picked up the blue of his eyes. It really wasn't cold enough for a heavy jacket, but I think Morgan knew he looked good in it.

"Hi, Morgan," said Katy brightly, nudging me.

"Hi," I muttered. It was all I could get out. My throat seemed to have closed up. Why was I always so nervous around Morgan?

"What are you doing here, Morgan?" Katy asked, swinging her ballet bag around.

I clutched my bag to my chest and stole glances at Morgan. I wished that I could have said anything—anything at all.

"I bought some sheet music for *Circus Town*. You know, that's the school musical," Morgan said. "I'm trying out for the role of the Ringmaster. You two are dancers, so you'll be trying out, right?"

This was the first I'd ever heard of the musical. But there is no way I'd try out. Madame Maur had been trying to get me into ballet recitals for years. But I have this problem with throwing up whenever I see a stage.

"Oh, we're not sure yet," Katy lied smoothly. I knew she hadn't heard about the musical herself, or she would have told me. "There are so many parts to choose from." Then she said, "By the way, I really like your jacket."

"Thanks," Morgan said. "It keeps me warm when I ski. Well, I have to run," he added, looking straight at me. I could feel my face flame. Why couldn't I think of something to say?

Katy kicked me again. Morgan flashed a

24

megawatt smile, waved, and walked down the street.

"See? It's easy to talk to a boy," she said. "You just compliment him on something. And see what happens? We learned something new about Morgan. He likes to ski."

"That's easy for you to say," I muttered. "In case you didn't notice, I couldn't say a word in front of him. He was talking to you. He doesn't even realize I exist."

"That's it!" Katy said. "I've figured out the perfect way to get Morgan to notice you! You'll try out for the play. We're going to have to get scripts and music and—"

"Oh, no," I groaned. "Have you forgotten that in second grade I threw up all over my Sugarplum Fairy costume just before *The Nutcracker?*"

Katy laughed. "Oh, don't be ridiculous. That was years ago. Here comes my mom."

Mrs. Provender drove her shiny, burgundy car up to the curb, and we climbed in. My head was still spinning from seeing Morgan, so I wasn't prepared for Katy's next move. She hadn't mentioned the stepmonsters all afternoon, so I had figured she'd forgotten about Justin and her plans to walk the dog. But I was wrong.

"Mom, can I go over to Kerri's?" Katy asked,

tossing her ballet bag on the floor of the front seat. "I have something I need to do."

I looked at her with questioning eyes.

"I'm going to walk Justin's dog," Katy whispered.

I snorted. Mrs. Provender didn't notice.

"Sure, dear," she said. "Just be home in time for dinner."

"I still don't get it," I said to Katy as we walked up the front walk together. "Why do you want to walk Justin's dumb dog so much?"

Katy shrugged. "You obviously don't want to, so I'm helping you out. What are friends for?"

"It's just because you like Justin," I said accusingly.

"So what? You like Morgan Granger. I don't give you a hard time about that, do I?" Katy pointed out. "In fact, I'm trying to help you."

"Forget about the musical, because there's no way I'll try out. And we don't know anything about it, anyway."

"No, but we can find out about it," Katy answered excitedly.

"Don't even think about it," I cautioned her.

Three

"I don't know how I'm going to make it through this week," I moaned as I watched Katy snap Digger's leash to his collar. Just seeing Digger reminded me of all the changes that were taking place in my life.

Katy only laughed, her red hair bouncing around her like it always did when she got excited about something.

"This is serious!" I practically yelled at her.

"Oh, don't be so serious," Katy said. "Ker, you're much too serious about things."

Katy was right. I was serious. And I didn't like changes, not even little ones.

"Get your nose out of my armpit this minute!" I snapped at Digger as he poked and prodded with his face. His whole body was wriggling in anticipation of his walk.

Katy pulled him back and looked at me. "Cheer up. Things will get better when your

27

parents come home," she said.

*The*y are not my parents," I said quickly. "Mom's mom, and Gary is—well—just Gary."

Even so, I couldn't wait for them to get home, I thought as I watched Katy step out the front door behind my stepmonsters' dog. Katy returned half an hour later, with Digger looking worn out and satisfied. Katy just wore a little smile of contentment. *Maybe I'd be happy, too, if this was happening to her family,* I thought.

Mom and Gary arrived home with armfuls of presents for everybody. She even had one for Aunt Sybil. My favorite was a Mexican doll that was dressed in an authentic dress, moccasins, and a sombrero. Having Mom home gave me only a short-lived thrill, since two days later was the big day, *moving day.*

I could barely sleep the night before, knowing that the stepmonsters would be in *my* house from now on. I woke up that morning to the sounds of screeching brakes and gravel crunching. Then loud rock music began blaring. I ran to my window and pulled back the lace curtains so that I could see what such a noise could be at this early hour.

Just as I figured, it was the stepmonsters. They all were piled in a very large moving truck, which had MOVE IT! written all over the sides. To go with the slogan was a huge picture of little ants carrying boxes on their backs. *Pretty dumb, huh?*

The changes were happening already. The boys were moving in today. I tried frantically to think about the talk that my mom and I had when she'd first gotten home from her honeymoon. She made me feel better with just a few words, but I couldn't remember any of them now. Feeling exhausted, I plodded back to bed and pulled the covers over my head to keep the day from beginning.

But before I knew it, I heard Mom's cheery voice call upstairs. "Rise and shine, Kerri. I've cooked pancakes for everyone. Let's go! We may not have another chance to eat all day during the move." Mom was using what I call her Miss Sunshine voice.

I hate that voice, because it usually means that I have to do something I'd rather not do. Today it meant getting up and eating breakfast with the stepmonsters. I heard a loud crash and someone shouting, "Hey, dummy, look out!"

"Don't those guys know that some people are still asleep at this hour?" I grumbled. "And how did they get up and pack so early?"

"Kerri," my mom said in a more severe tone, "it's almost 10:30. It's time to get going!"

Something told me that I'd better move it. Pulling on a grungy, old sweatshirt and shoving my shoes on my sockless feet, I started down to breakfast just as I did normally.

Then I remembered that there would be boys at the breakfast table from now on. They were only stepmonsters, but they were boys. I went back to the closet for a change of clothes. I put on my new teddy bear sweatshirt and clean jeans. A few minutes later, I headed for my usual place at the antique, pine breakfast table, but someone was sitting there already. It was Justin.

I glared at him, and then I walked to the refrigerator to get some milk. I slammed the door harder than was necessary and plunked my glass down angrily on the counter.

Gary looked up at me. "Is something wrong?" he asked.

"Well, it's just that Justin's sitting in my chair," I mumbled.

"There are other chairs," Justin commented and nodded in the direction of the empty chair next to him.

"That's my chair," I repeated stiffly, looking toward my mother for help. She remained silent.

"Justin, move over so Kerri can sit there," said Gary quickly.

"Justin was there first," said Blake loudly.

"That's right," said Justin.

"Let's step out to the family room and talk, Justin," Gary ordered. "Now."

My mom shot me a look as Justin got up, but I didn't care. Who did this guy think he was, anyway? He deserved a lecture.

I sat down and didn't look at anyone while I poured syrup on my pancakes. Justin and Gary reappeared a moment later, and Justin took a seat next to me.

I looked around the table. Justin was scowling at his breakfast. What a grump he was. I couldn't believe he was upset about a stupid chair. I had never heard Tim say much to anyone about anything. He just sat quietly and watched people. Blake was singing to himself as he ran his finger around and around on his pancakes to spread his butter. *Gross! Why didn't Gary say something to make him stop?*

"Why do Blake and I have to share a room?" asked Tim.

"We've already been through this," Gary said. "Justin's the oldest."

"Being the oldest shouldn't matter," Tim persisted. He looked at me.

"But it does," I said, because he seemed to expect an answer from me.

"It's really none of your business," Justin snapped at me angrily.

"Pass the syrup, please," Blake piped up just then.

The container that Mom always uses for syrup was in front of me, so I passed it. Blake picked it up and then dumped it all over the table. A long, sticky trail seeped onto our blue and white checked tablecloth.

I watched my mom's face take in the drippy mess for a second. She would have sighed and demanded that I clean it up if I'd been the one to dump the syrup. But what did she do now? She just laughed, got up, ruffled Blake's hair like he'd gotten 100 percent on an English test, and reached for a sponge.

I scowled while Mom tried to soak up the mess, and Blake glopped what was left of the syrup onto his pancakes. No one except Tim said anything after that, and he kept up a running stream of humming noises.

"So, Kerri, are you feeling strong today?" Gary blurted as he shoveled the last forkful of pancake into his mouth and reached for his coffee to wash it down. "We need some help with all of the stuff we've carted over here."

"Huh? I guess so," I said, still cutting into my first pancake.

"Are you kidding, Dad? She's a girl," said

Blake. "She won't be able to carry anything."

"You'd be surprised at how strong a girl she is," Mom said as she returned to her seat. "The dancing she does builds muscles."

Tim looked at me carefully. It made me feel weird, like he had X-ray eyes or something and could see into my brain.

"Well, Kerri doesn't look very strong," Tim said.

"See my muscles?" I asked, rolling up the sleeves of my teddy bear sweatshirt for his benefit. Mom was right. All my dance classes hadn't been for nothing.

"You've got chicken wings," teased Justin.

"Enough talk," said Gary loudly as he pushed back his chair and stood up. "We've got some moving to do."

"Katy said she'd come over to help, too," I said, as I got up and stacked my plate in the sink.

As we went out to the truck, I saw Katy walking up the street. "I'm glad you're here," I whispered to her so that no one else would hear.

Katy smiled and shrugged. "Where do we start?"

We all started hauling odds and ends down the ramp, and there were lots of them! I counted at least four mud-splattered bikes

33

and Gary's motorcycle. Then came lots of Blake's toys. Blake, Mom, and Katy carried them to the bedroom that he was going to share with Tim.

"Their mother spoils them rotten," Gary said to Mom as she came back for the fourth armful of toys.

I froze. *How could Mom not mind Gary talking about his ex-wife, now that she is his wife?* Mom just smiled. Grown-ups are strange at times. I shook my head.

"Here, I'll take that," I offered as Gary got ready to hand a big roll of carpet to Justin. I would show them all that I didn't have chicken wings for arms.

"Oooof," I grunted as the full weight of the carpet fell against me. "Where does it go?"

"In the family room," offered Mom.

"Need any help?" offered Justin, grinning wickedly at me as I staggered.

"No, thanks," I said. "But let me know if *you* need any help." Wrapping my arms around the bulky carpet, I dragged and kicked it up the walkway toward the house. I almost killed myself when I tripped neatly over Digger and fell heavily onto the grass next to the walk. Digger barked with delight and licked my face. I wanted to scream.

It was Justin who rushed to my side and

pushed Digger away. "Stop provoking my dog!" he snapped at me.

I glared at him. "Put your dog back in the backyard where he belongs," I growled as I got up and dusted myself off. Then I finally maneuvered the carpet through the front door and into the house.

Katy had to go home after lunch. The rest of us kept unpacking without another break until late afternoon. You wouldn't believe how much junk those guys have. I wondered what Mom would say about their slick, modern stuff in our country house.

"Please take this box up to Blake's room, and then go rest a few minutes," Mom said as she watched me wrestle with the box. Its bottom kept falling open, spilling marbles and toys everywhere.

Believe me, I didn't need a second invitation to take a break. I dumped off the box, and then I ducked into my room and sprawled onto my bed. My muscles were aching, so I turned on some music to start my stretching exercises. I was too tired to even change into my leotard, so I was hoping my routine would give me some energy.

I had just completed stretching on the ballet barre that Dad had built for me, when Mom knocked and came in.

35

"Sorry to interrupt, honey," she said, "but you're really going to need to get those stuffed animals out of the back bedroom closet. Believe me, Justin's going to need all the room he can get."

Uh-oh. Where in the world were all my stuffed animals going to go? My room was crowded as it was. It was negotiation time.

"Mom, just let me keep them there for a couple of weeks while I figure out what to do with them," I said as I reached over to switch off the stereo.

"You'll have to talk with Justin about that. It's his room now," Mom said, and then she disappeared down the hall.

"It's his room now," I mimicked almost to myself.

I was just starting down the hall to talk with Justin about the stuffed animals when the phone rang.

"I'll get it!" yelled Justin from his room.

"I'm closest," I said reaching the phone first and quickly grabbing the receiver.

A high-pitched girl's voice said, "Uh—hi— is this the Freeman residence?"

"Freeman? Sorry, you must have the wrong number," I said, trying to fend off Justin, who was trying to grab the phone. "This is the Rutherford residence. Good-bye."

"Why did you do that?" yelled Justin as I hung up. "We're the Freemans. We live here now, too remember?"

"Oh," I said in a small voice as I realized the truth of what Justin was saying. But then I got mad. I mean, anyone could make a mistake like that. "Well, big deal. She'll call back."

"Who was it?" Justin demanded, looking me in the eye. "If it was who I think it was, you're in trouble. I don't know if she'll call again or not."

"I don't know who it was," I said with a shrug. "It was some girl." Then another thought hit me. "Is she your girlfriend?"

"It's none of your business," Justin stated, and then he disappeared down the hall. "Next time make sure you don't hang up on my friends."

I stuck my tongue out at him as he walked back down the hall. He didn't see me, but it made me feel better. I decided any negotiation with Justin wasn't worth it. I would go ahead and move my stuffed animals.

Later that afternoon, I came out of my room to grab a sandwich, and I almost met head-on with disaster. I looked up just before I smashed into a large bookshelf that Tim and Justin were carrying down the hall.

"Did you decide to help again?" asked Justin as the bookshelf came to a stop. He gave me an annoyed look. It was a very different look than the one he'd used when he begged me to take his dog for a week.

Blake came up behind him. "Excuse me, you're in my way," he said to me.

"You're in our way," Tim echoed, glaring at me. I looked at him for a long moment while a range of emotions flooded through me. I couldn't speak because tears started bubbling up in my throat.

That did it. Who were these three boys to stand in *my* hall and tell me that I was in *their* way?

"You *all* are in my way!" I said coldly.

Hearing the commotion, Digger ran down the hallway to see what the noise was. The dumb dog must have forgotten that only minutes before, he'd been licking my face. He forgot that it was me who took pity on him and took him in when he had nowhere to go. *That dumb dog actually growled at me!*

Four

ON Monday morning, I managed to sleep right through the alarm. I had set it to wake me up a little early so that I could study before school. When I finally woke up, I jumped out of bed and jammed on my slippers.

"Ugh, an English test today," I mumbled to Percy, who was yawning and stretching on the bed. English and I do not get along. "I'd better hurry."

But when I got to the bathroom, I was surprised to find the door locked. The sound of the running shower greeted my ears.

"Oh," I said aloud. Sharing the bathroom was a problem that hadn't occurred to me before the stepmonsters moved in. I was already running late, and I hoped that whoever was in there wouldn't take too long. I knocked on the door. There was no response. Then the blow dryer started whirring.

"Hurry up in there!" I shouted to the closed door. Again, there was no response.

After what seemed like an eternity, the door opened, and Justin came out. His hair was styled perfectly. He was dressed in black cords and a yellow shirt.

"Boy, are you impatient! Do you think you're the only one who lives here?" he exclaimed, glaring at me.

I ignored him and rushed into the bathroom. Then I closed the door with a bang and locked it. I gasped as the lingering steam and heat from Justin's blow-dryer hit me in the face.

The bathroom looked like a disaster area. I stepped on a frayed toothbrush and a toothpaste container that I didn't recognize. Then I noticed a can of extra-strength mouthwash sitting on the counter.

I caught a glimpse of myself in the steamed-up mirror and watched my cheeks slowly turn red. *No big deal*, I told myself sternly. *It's just a bottle of mouthwash.* But still, seeing boy's stuff in *my* bathroom definitely was weird.

I showered quickly to make up for lost time. But halfway through the shower, I ran out of hot water. And I still had my hair to wash. As

I grabbed my shampoo bottle, I noticed that half of it was gone. *No trouble figuring out where it went*, I thought. As I reached for the fresh towel hanging on the rack, a big embroidered *F* on its center caught my eye. I dropped it in a heap and searched until I found my familiar, peach-striped towel.

After I'd dried my hair and gotten dressed, I was ready to face the world—and my English test. I was still smiling as I went down to breakfast. Mom was making lunch for Blake to take to school. Blake wouldn't eat his breakfast, so Gary was patting him on the back, telling him how much he would like his new school. I felt sorry for the little guy. I remembered how scared I was to start school, and I'd had the advantage of knowing quite a few kids. Even then, I'd thrown up the first day.

"Listen, Blake, I'll play trucks with you when I get home," I said in a moment of generosity. Offering to be nice to Blake would show Mom and Gary that I could be a good sport.

Tim and Justin were already eating, although Tim seemed more absorbed in playing some game on the back of the cereal box than in eating. I noticed that Tim was still in his pajamas, but I didn't say anything. Gary mentioned it, though, and ordered Tim to stop playing around and to go shower.

I poured a bowl of cereal and began eating just as Justin finished his with one noisy slurp.

"I'm going out to dunk a few," he said. He picked up a basketball that had been under his chair, and he and Digger went outside. My stepmonsters had put a basketball hoop up on the garage, and through the window I watched Justin shoot a few baskets as I ate the last of my cereal.

"Kerri," Mom said, while I loaded my bowl into the dishwasher. *Uh-oh*, I thought, *here comes the Miss Sunshine voice.*

"Hmmm?" I mumbled warily.

"You will show Justin around school, won't you? After all, remember how difficult it can be when you're new."

"Oh, sure," I said with a shrug as I reached for my notebook.

"I don't want to be new," blurted Blake, and he started to cry.

"You'll be all right," I said and gave him a hug.

I started down the driveway and tried to ignore the nonstop *plumpph, plumpph* of the basketball that Justin was dribbling behind me. *Was he going to follow me with that stupid*

42

ball all the way to school? I wondered. I didn't turn around to look back. *Okay so I'd agreed to show him around at school, but that promise didn't take effect until we stepped onto school grounds.*

But as we crossed the street in front of San Martin Junior High, Justin came up next to me. He tossed the ball back and forth in his hands.

"So, you've decided not to talk to me?" he asked in this tough voice. I noticed that his hair was a little out of place.

"We're almost at school, and hair number 344 is out of place," I remarked.

"Huh?" Justin reached up and smoothed his hair.

"Maybe you should have helped yourself to my hair spray as well as most of my shampoo," I snapped.

"Was that your shampoo?" asked Justin.

"Look, when we get to school, I'll take you to the main office, and the school secretary will give you your school schedule and a little map. I'm sure you'll find your way around just fine," I said. I shifted my books from one arm to the other.

"Aw, you're not still mad at me because I sat in your chair the other day at breakfast, are you?" Justin asked.

That and a million other things, I thought to myself. I raised my eyebrows coolly, the way I thought a prima ballerina might.

"Well, that's ridiculous. I moved for you, didn't I?" he persisted. "Anyway, I'm not going to hate your guts forever, even though you hung up on my friend, Julie."

"Sorry about that," I said grudgingly. I wondered about Julie for a minute. I guess she reminded me that Justin really did have another life somewhere else before he and his family moved to San Luis Obispo to live with us.

"Is Julie your girlfriend?" I asked.

"She was, if you really must know. But then we had to move here," Justin said disgustedly.

"San Luis Obispo's a nice place," I said, rushing to the defense of my hometown.

Justin rolled his eyes and kept dribbling.

When we arrived at school, I pointed the way to the school secretary's office. *There, I've done my duty*, I thought as I started to walk off.

"See ya around," Justin said.

I saw him standing there, looking like a lost puppy for a minute. For a split second, I almost gave in and turned to walk him to the office. That is, until he grinned at me and said, "Your slip's showing, Sis." Just like that—out loud—in front of everyone.

"I'm not your sis," I replied, checking my slip at the same time and tugging at my waistband. I spun around and headed down the hall. By the time I got to first period, I had thought of a million tortures I'd like to perform on him. *What a jerk!*

Despite what Justin had said, though, by the time I slid into my seat for second-period history class, I did feel a little guilty about abandoning him. I wasn't usually a creep.

I began worrying about how Blake was doing at his new school. And I wondered if Tim got off to school in time. Geez! I was doing all this worrying over my stepmonsters who had done nothing but bug me from the day they moved into my life. I decided then and there that I wouldn't waste another minute thinking about them.

It turned out that I shouldn't have wasted a second feeling bad about Justin. By lunch period, at least three girls in my classes had asked me who the cute new guy was. Could they possibly be talking about Justin? *No way,* I thought. They must have been talking about some other new guy.

At lunch, I caught a glimpse of Justin in the cafeteria sitting with a large, noisy group

45

of kids from student council. Two of the girls actually raced each other to sit beside Justin. Tiffani Pearlman gave each of those two a frozen smile and quickly slipped her tray next to Justin's and sat down. *So much for the poor lost puppy,* I thought. Things seemed to be going very smoothly for Justin.

"Hey, isn't that Justin?" asked Katy as she and Ashley Klemper set their trays next to mine. She flipped back her ponytail in this weird way that she has, and her eyes lighted up. "Look. He's eating with the *in* crowd. Isn't he sitting next to Tiffani Pearlman?"

The popular crowd was a sore spot with me. When Katy and I had begun junior high, we'd slowly become friends with some of the kids on the student council. It seemed like we'd been accepted, which was terrific since Morgan Granger was part of that crowd. Then, Tiffani Pearlman had moved to San Luis Obispo, and she quickly zeroed in on the popular crowd—and Morgan. She also took an instant dislike to me. She made her move, and before I knew it, Tiffani was part of the *in* crowd with Morgan. Just as suddenly, it seemed, I was out again.

It wasn't that I minded my crowd of friends. Ashley, Meghan, and Katy were the best. But I would have loved being part of *that* crowd.

46

Katy and I pretended that all of those kids were shallow, but we'd have given anything to be one of the popular kids.

So, here was Justin on his first day of school. He'd already bewitched Tiffani and taken over the cool crowd like he owned the school.

"Yes, it's Justin, and he can have that crowd," I finally muttered, toying with my straw and wishing that it was a missile. I knew precisely where I'd like to send it.

"Tiffani's sitting right next to him," Katy repeated.

"Yeah, so what if she is?" I asked in disgust.

"I just wish she weren't so pretty," Katy muttered. "Look who's sitting next to her on the other side. It's Morgan Granger."

"So what?" I asked casually, but my eyes slid over to take a good look for myself.

"Don't give me *so what*," Katy said. "You like him. So let him know." She always said that to me.

"Give me a break," I replied as I always did. "He's totally good looking. He hangs out with the cool crowd. And he doesn't even know that Kerri Rutherford exists."

"I already told you that he would if you tried out for the school musical," Katy said lightly. She turned to Ashley.

"Do you know anything about the musical that's coming up?"

I turned away and played with my food.

"The lead character is Alicia," Ashley said. "She gets to dance a lot."

"Are you kidding?" I interrupted. "I could never be a lead in a play. Madame Maur has never been able to get me into a dance recital. I'd have an attack of shyness or throw up, and you'd have to carry me off the stage."

"Oh, that would never happen. You've come a long way since the time we danced *The Nutcracker*," Katy said. "Anyway, imagine if Morgan was the one to carry you off the stage."

"Talk about humiliating," I said. "That settles it. Just forget the idea of me trying out."

"Okay, for now, but I'm not giving up. So, what's it like to live in a house full of guys, especially Justin?" Katy's eyes brightened with anticipation.

"Justin uses a blow-dryer to fix his hair," I confided in a low voice.

Katy threw her head back and laughed. "He does?" she shrieked. "Mr. Rough and Tough BMXer?"

Then we both cracked up. "And he squeezes the tooth gel from the middle of the

48

tube. He also used up most of the bottle of my springtime-scented shampoo this morning," I added.

Meghan and some other girls in our group came over and sat down. "Guess what?" asked Meghan the second that she had plopped on the bench next to Katy. "Mr. Reynolds just moved the date of the tryouts for the musical to next week. I want the part of the Beautiful Lady. I just saw some drawings of her costume this morning in Ms. Nash's home economics room."

"Could it be that you heard that Michael Stewart is trying out for the Thin Man who's madly in love with the Beautiful Lady?" Ashley teased.

"Maybe. Michael's a nice guy. Oh, it's going to be so romantic," Meghan said with a dramatic sigh.

"The important question is whether any other guys try out to be the dancing partners?" Ashley asked.

"Are you kidding?" asked Katy. "That new dancing movie has made all the guys think that they are dancing dynamos. Did you hear that Michael Stewart is even making a dance video in his garage?"

We all laughed. At the school dance we'd had last fall, hardly any of the guys would get out and dance. But one hot dancing movie later, and guys were making dance videos in their garages!

"Which part gets to dance the most?" I asked, trying not to appear too interested. But I knew I didn't fool anyone.

"It's Alicia," said Ashley. "I think you'd be great since you're such a good dancer. And if Morgan Granger is the Ringmaster—wow! Just think of it."

I clutched at my throat in an exaggerated death grasp. "Me, try out for the lead in front of all those people? Anyway, wouldn't you figure that Tiffani is trying out for Alicia, too?"

"So, what if she is?" was Katy's comeback. "You're prettier and a better dancer. You've got to stop being so shy. Fight for the part."

"I wish it were that easy," I said, toying with my straw wrapper some more. But inside, the idea of being Alicia, dancing, and having Morgan notice me was making me dizzy.

"Katy, you should try out for Clarissa," said Ashley. "She has almost as many speaking parts as Alicia. But she's funnier and tells the worst jokes."

"That settles it," Katy said. "I will!"

"Are you ever shy?" I asked Katy. Even though we'd been friends for years, her outgoing personality never failed to amaze me. She would try anything.

"Nope," Katy answered, her green eyes twinkling. "Why be shy when you've got brains and beauty both on your side?"

We all laughed. It was impossible not to crack up whenever Katy laughed.

"Here, take my script and read it tonight," Ashley said to me. "Just bring it back tomorrow."

Don't ask me why, but I took it. During my last class, we had a substitute teacher who gave us free time to catch up on our work. I used the time to read through the script, and I was so intrigued that I began seeing myself in Alicia's gorgeous costume.

Could I actually do it? Could I actually try out for the part of Alicia? It was going to take bravery galore to try out against the girls of the *in* crowd. Still, the possibility of Morgan as the lead was reason enough to try. The bell rang, and I began the walk home, toying with visions of Alicia the whole way.

The minute I slipped through the kitchen door, Blake and Digger came running up to me. This time Digger didn't growl. Instead, he drooled all over my new tennis shoes.

"Hey, you stupid dog. Now I'll have to wash these," I said, pushing him away.

"Will you play trucks with me, or read me

a story?" Blake asked, tugging at my sleeve.

"Not now," I said absently, reaching into the refrigerator for an apple.

"Please?" Blake persisted. His blue eyes looked up at me.

"Where's my mom?" I asked. She was usually home by now from the design studio. Who did Blake think I was, his baby-sitter?

Just then Tim came into the kitchen. He had a screwdriver in his hand. "Anita (the boys called Mom by her first name) called to say that she'd be late. Is there anything to eat in here? I've been fixing my bike, and I'm starved," he said, looking at me expectantly.

I shrugged. "There are some apples in the refrigerator," I said.

"No, I mean real food," Tim said. "I mean stuff like twinkies, doughnuts, pizza."

"How should I know? I never eat anything besides an apple after school, or I'll gain weight and hurt my ballet," I said.

"Ballet? How boring," sneered Tim. "Justin's into cool dancing. What can you do with ballet? I hear you're too chicken to go on stage, anyway."

"Dancing's a lot more interesting than riding stupid bikes around in the mud," I said. "And I'm not chicken. I'm trying out for the role of Alicia, the lead in the school musical.

That's what I can do with my dancing." I couldn't believe I'd just said that. Two days ago, I didn't know anything about a school musical. I hated being in front of an audience. And here I was, telling Tim that I was going on stage to try out for the lead part.

"Please read me a story," Blake begged.

"Oh, all right," I muttered, casting a reluctant look at my script, my head still dizzy over my snap decision.

"Hey, don't bother," Tim suddenly said. "*I'm* his brother. *I'll* read a story to him."

Blake said, "Kerri's my sister now. Dad said so. She can read me a story." Then he slipped his little hand in mine.

"She's not your real sister," Tim said.

Blake looked at us in confusion. Then he burst into tears and ran out of the kitchen. Tim followed him.

I grabbed my apple and stomped upstairs to my room, clicking the door shut behind me. This was getting crazier by the second! These guys had been in my house for only a week, and all they did was pick fights with me.

I tossed the script on the floor and sat staring at my wall, tracing the pattern of the floral wallpaper with my eyes. At least I still had my room, my own special place where I could get away from everything.

Then the phone rang. I sprang for it. The caller was a guy for Justin. I yelled down the hall to Justin, and he barreled out of his room and grabbed the phone from me like I was going to hang up again.

A few minutes later, there was another phone call for Justin. This time, it was a call from Tiffani.

"Hi, Kerri," said Tiffani in a sugary voice. "Is Justin there?"

I made a face at the receiver before handing the phone to Justin.

I went back to my room, shut the door, and began reading through the script again. I was awakened from deep thought by the intense vibrations that were coming through the wall. *THUGG-A, THUGG-A, THUMP. THUGG-A, THUGG-A, THUMP.* It was Justin's stereo. I jumped up off my bed and marched down the hall.

"Can you turn it down?" I asked loudly over the deafening roar. Justin had kicked away the rug from the center of the room, and was jerking and twisting to what sounded like metal grating against a blackboard. He gave one huge convulsive leap into the air and threw his arms dramatically toward me.

"No, I won't. It's the Pantyhose from Mars!" shouted Justin. He resumed his jerking and twisting around the room.

I was shocked. "What did you call me?"

Justin's face broke out in a big grin. "I didn't call you anything. I said this is the Pantyhose from Mars, the rock group. Aren't they great?"

"If you like this kind of music," I answered, but I didn't think Justin could hear a word I said.

"Did you ever learn this in ballet?" he asked as he leaped into the air, landing on one foot with the other raised behind. It looked like a jete that I might do in ballet class, except he bent his knee and opened his hands wide.

I rolled my eyes. His dancing was elementary stuff. But then again, most of the guys I knew didn't move even that well.

"Where'd you learn to do that?" I shouted.

"Oh, I took some dance classes a couple of years ago. The coach said it might help my basketball," Justin shouted back. "Anyway, it might come in handy when I have my own rock band someday."

He finally stopped and turned the stereo down. Even he finally realized it was impossible to talk with that thing blasting. I took a swift glance around his room. In only a week, he had completely changed the place. Gone were the guest bed, my stuffed animals, and the sentimental country things that my mom had set across the dresser. Now the room was overflowing with stereo equipment, rock posters, and computer stuff. Justin's bike hung from a weird contraption that was attached to the ceiling.

"Does Mom know you put that thing on your ceiling?" I asked.

Justin explained reluctantly. I could tell he just wished I'd get out of his room, but something made me stay. Maybe it was just because this used to be the guest room, and I felt that I could stay in it as long as I wanted. Just then, Blake wandered into the room still carrying his book.

"Will you read to me, Kerri? Tim reads funny," Blake said. "His voice gets all weird when he reads the littlest truck's part."

"Sure," I said. Blake jumped on Justin's bed and settled down for the story. I glanced at Justin, and he shrugged. His look seemed to say that I could stay.

I sat cross-legged on the floor and began to read. I suddenly felt kind of warm inside. I couldn't explain it, but I was glad that Tim read funny. And for a few minutes, I could even forgive Justin for taking over my house and my school. I was enjoying the warmth of a house full of people and the weird, soft background sounds of the Pantyhose from Mars.

Instant family, I thought to myself. *Just add water.* And part of me was thinking, *Well, why not?*

Five

THE next morning, I woke up before the alarm went off. Settling back into my pillow, I closed my eyes lazily and pictured myself in Alicia's sparkly, satin costume. Morgan stepped into my vision and held out his arms to me. I imagined him taking me in his strong arms and holding me close.

My eyes flew open. *It would never happen. Don't even think about it,* I grumbled to myself, and then I threw back the covers. But it could if I could get up the courage to try out for the part of Alicia.

By moving quickly, I managed to beat Justin to the bathroom. I was dressed and ready to leave for school before he'd even finished blow-drying his hair. *Score one for me,* I thought gleefully as I slid into my chair at breakfast.

I thought about the tryouts and Morgan

while I poured my milk into my cereal. Again, I pictured Morgan actually noticing me. That thought pushed away my nervousness, and I started to feel kind of hopeful about the whole thing. I felt so encouraged that I helped Blake pour the milk onto his cereal and smiled at him across the table. Gary was hiding behind his newspaper, or I would have smiled at him, too.

"Hey, Kerri," called Tim as he reached for a slice of toast. "Did you notice that I fixed your old bike last night?"

"You did?" I blinked. "I don't ride my bike anymore."

"You can ride it now. I fixed it. The gears needed some work. I did it while you were reading," Tim said. I noticed that once again he was wearing his pajamas at the breakfast table.

"Wasn't that nice of him, dear?" Mom chimed in. "These boys really know bikes."

"Yeah, Tim spent a lot of time on that," said Justin as he walked into the kitchen. "The least you can do is say thanks."

I shot an icy look at him until I saw Mom's expression. I mumbled my thanks. Tim didn't appear to notice. He was already immersed in some pocket video game that he'd brought to the breakfast table. Gary had to tell him twice to put it down and to take a shower.

Justin gulped down his glass of orange juice without even bothering to sit at the table.

"You used up all the hot water," he said to me accusingly. I didn't answer.

"Justin, back off," Gary said in a warning tone.

"Let's go," Justin said to me as he set down his empty glass and wiped the sleeve of his jacket across his mouth.

"Aren't you going to eat anything?" Mom asked worriedly.

"No," Justin replied as he gathered his books.

"Yes, he is," said Gary sternly. I was glad Gary never spoke to me like that. I'd noticed he was pretty strict with the boys, especially Justin.

"Uh, sure," Justin scowled, and then he looked around the table and grabbed an apple out of the fruit bowl. He shoved it into his pocket. "Let's go."

When we got out to the street, he tossed the apple into the gutter. We watched it roll a few times before it came to rest next to a soggy leaf pile.

"I hate eating breakfast," Justin said with an intensity that startled me. "I wish your mom hadn't made a big deal out of it."

"My mom didn't make a big deal out of it. She just asked you a question. If you ask me, it was your dad who made the big deal," I snapped. All of my good feelings of the morning were rolling away just as the apple had.

"Your mom started it," Justin said sullenly.

"She did not," I said in her defense.

"She did, too," he repeated.

I looked at him, not giving an inch. After all, I was sure that I was right. It seemed like Gary was always the heavy, not like the way *my* dad used to be. My mom prefers trying to ease you into doing things that you don't want to do.

Justin stomped on ahead, and I waited a few minutes so we wouldn't have to walk to school together. I walked along reading my script, which got tricky since I tripped over three curbs before I got to school.

When I stepped onto the grounds, the first thing I saw was Justin standing with Tiffani and her friends by the flagpole. I walked past them as quickly as possible without looking at Justin.

At lunchtime, my friends and I met up at our usual table.

"El yucko! Pizza rounds again?" Katy cried, eyeing her lunch tray.

"I'm so nervous about the audition that I won't even taste it," Meghan said as soon as she sat down and dumped her books on top of mine. She held out her nibbled fingernails to me as proof.

"Me, too," I said softly.

Katy was on that comment in an instant. "So, Kerri, does that mean you're trying out for the part of Alicia?" she asked eagerly.

I took a huge bite of rubbery pizza and swallowed. I thought of Morgan. "Yeah, I'm trying out for Alicia. I may die, but I'm going to try out."

"Good for you. I know you can do it. Just don't worry. You're such a great dancer, no one will ever notice that you're nervous," Katy said and then turned to the others.

I slugged Katy playfully in the shoulder and felt my face go pink. I did feel better knowing that Katy thought I'd survive tryouts.

Suddenly, Katy sucked in her breath. "Don't look now, but here comes Justin," she said in a tone of voice normally reserved for rock stars. "He sure is cute in that rugby shirt."

Any warmth I had just felt toward Katy instantly vanished as I followed her gaze. There he was, surrounded by Tiffani, of course, and some others, including Morgan.

They all made their way toward the cool table. Justin glanced my way and then quickly turned away.

"He's not cute," I muttered, thinking how un-cute Justin looked that morning when he made a big deal about my mom wanting him to eat breakfast.

I stole another look at Morgan. Now *he* was the cute one, with his wavy brown hair and electric blue eyes. Tiffani sure was lucky, but she didn't seem to know a good guy when she had him. Morgan sat down next to her. The two of them were sitting so close that they seemed to be glued together, but Tiffani's attention was directed toward Justin.

"Are you kidding? Look at that smile, and his eyes," Katy said. "He was sitting behind me in science class this morning. And when he said something to me, I almost dropped my pond water full of amoebas. Did you know that we have science class together?"

"Huh?" I was still thinking of Morgan. "Justin's an amoeba," I said to Katy. "Get a grip on yourself," I added.

Katy didn't hear me. She continued eyeing Justin as he ate lunch. *If only Mom could see him now*, I thought. Besides his own pizza round, he ate Tiffani's and her friend Terri Dunlop's, and he drank at least three cartons of milk. Mom didn't have to worry about Justin starving.

I told my friends that I had to go to the library to work on a project, but I actually went to Mr. Reynolds' room to get my own script. I didn't have any time to waste.

I was excited about having the weekend to practice in peace. Early Saturday morning, the boys packed up some clothes and went to their mom's house. Our house did feel strangely empty without them, but it was nice. I stayed in the bathroom as long as I wanted, and no one bugged me about using up all the hot water.

On Sunday, Mom went to some design show, so Katy and I practiced our parts at her house. That evening when I got home, I nearly broke my neck tripping over a huge box that was sitting just inside the kitchen door. The description on the box said that it was a color TV.

"Wow! What's this?" I sucked in my breath and crouched down to examine the box.

"It's mine," Justin said angrily as he came into the kitchen. He kicked the box lightly with a sneakered toe. "My mom bought it for me. She bought Tim a new monitor for his computer and practically the whole toy store for Blake."

"Well, don't worry. I won't touch your TV," I said.

"You can have it," Justin snapped. "It doesn't mean anything to me. I wish Mom hadn't bought it."

"You wish she hadn't bought you a new TV? Are you out of your mind?" I asked.

"I don't watch TV much," snapped Justin.

I shook my head and headed for my room. *Justin sure was a strange guy*, I mused to myself as I walked up the stairs. At home he was a total grump, but at school he was the life of the party. And then there was the TV. If someone gave me a present like that, I surely wouldn't mind. I pushed aside thoughts of Justin's weirdness, and I began attacking the pile of homework that was growing on my desk.

* * * * *

For the next five days, I ate, slept, breathed, and dreamed the role of Alicia. The dance parts were much easier than anything we did at Madame Maur's, but Alicia's character was pretty complicated.

I changed my mind about trying out for Alicia a hundred times. I kept thinking about throwing up during *The Nutcracker*, but my daydreams always came back to Morgan. Maybe he'd never really notice plain Kerri Rutherford, but he'd just have to notice glamorous Alicia, the star of the circus.

A week later, I stood in the wings of the stage waiting for my name to be called from the tryout roster. The butterflies in my stomach were dancing already, but I felt amazingly excited. Mr. Reynolds finally called my name, and I stepped out onto the stage before him and the school principal, Mr. Richert.

As I read Alicia's lines and did a dance number, I tried to focus on what I was doing. That way, I wouldn't think about throwing up, or about the cool stares that Tiffani had been giving me ever since she had heard that I was trying out. I tried to think only of Morgan and how he'd notice me if I got the part.

"You were great. Tiffani will never get it," Katy whispered to me as we slipped out of the auditorium after we'd both tried out. "She couldn't act like a nice person like Alicia if she tried. And she can't dance at all."

I threw Katy a weak smile. Tiffani had looked pretty for her tryout. Maybe Mr. Reynolds wouldn't care that she wasn't a dancer. Maybe he'd think that she and Morgan would make a perfect stage couple.

Katy and I walked, both of us deep in thought, to our locker and dumped our books in it. I slammed the locker door shut, and we both spun around as we heard someone's footsteps echoing in the empty hallway. It was Morgan. He must have just finished his audition, too.

My heart froze in my chest as he casually walked by. I held my breath. "I didn't know you were going to try out for the lead, Kerri. Good luck," he said with a friendly wave. "I hope you get it."

I couldn't believe my ears. I think my heart stopped for a few seconds.

"See, Kerri? Just by auditioning, you got Morgan's attention!" Katy said excitedly as soon as he was out of earshot. "And he said that he hopes you get the part!"

Maybe Katy was right, I thought. Now I worried more than ever about Tiffani getting *my* part. I didn't think I could stand her being with Morgan.

I was dying to know if I got the part. I certainly could forget about sleeping tonight.

* * * * *

"You got it! You got it!" Katy squealed the next day. We were part of a large group that was crowded around the tryout sheet, which Mr. Reynolds had just posted on his door. Tiffani and her friends walked up right behind us. I looked at the list. Sure enough, there was my name next to the part of Alicia. And Morgan Granger would be playing the Ringmaster. *He'd have to notice me now!* I thought. If only I could get over my shyness and play the part.

"And I got Clarissa," Katy went on. Her red, curly hair rippled as she bounced up and down. Clarissa was the girl who'd just joined the circus, and who becomes friends with Alicia in the first act. I forgot about Morgan as we both jumped up and down and hugged each other. I tried not to notice the mean look that Tiffani shot me when she realized that she had lost out on the lead.

"Oh, I have the Beautiful Lady's part," Tiffani said, scanning the list and tossing back her hair. "Congratulations, Kerri," she added. But it was obvious that she didn't mean it. "And don't get excited about being with Morgan because he knows who his friends are."

I ignored Tiffani, but then I realized that if Tiffani got that part, Meghan hadn't. Still, I noted with relief that Meghan had gotten the Tatooed Lady role, which had a few speaking lines. My thoughts were interrupted by loud laughter as the guys read off the list of the male dancers.

"Hey, don't disappear so fast, Michael," said one guy. "You're not just in the chorus. You've got a big part with lots of dancing."

Michael Stewart wailed, "But that means I have to memorize lines. Maybe I shouldn't have tried out. I should have known Mr. Reynolds would stick me with a speaking part."

Just then Mr. Reynolds opened the door.

"I see the cast has gathered," he said with a smile. "Congratulations, everyone! And to those of you who don't have a stage part, your help is needed just as much in other areas." He then taped up a sign-up sheet for the stage crew, costume designers, and publicity committee. I watched as a few disappointed people put their names on the sheet.

"Our first rehearsal is tomorrow after school. It's important for everyone to be there," Mr. Reynolds said. Then he disappeared down the hallway.

The crowd was thinning when Meghan and Ashley went on to class. Tiffani deliberately elbowed me as she left. Katy and I stayed behind to read the cast list more thoroughly. Suddenly, I felt a basketball tap lightly on the top of my head.

It was Justin. He caught the ball neatly and started twirling it on his finger.

"Hi, Justin," Katy said. I stepped not so lightly on her toe. She kicked me back. If Justin noticed any of our fancy footwork, he ignored it.

"Oh, so you're the star," he said to me, scanning the cast list.

"Yeah, so what?" I asked, ready for a smart remark.

"I'm Clarissa," Katy added.

"I'm thinking about signing up for the stage crew," he said. "That way, I won't be left out," he added with a wink at Katy. "And, I can keep an eye on you, Sis," he said, winking at me.

"Why don't you join the basketball team or something else instead of the play?" I asked.

"Oh, I already have," Justin said coolly. "Or rather the basketball team chose me. So, don't act like you're the only one in the family who can accomplish anything."

"I never said I was," I protested. Justin was making me madder by the minute.

"That's great that you're on the team," Katy gushed.

"It's too bad my own sister doesn't think so," he said.

"I'm not your sister!" I shouted as I grabbed the basketball from Justin and threw it back at him. He caught it easily and laughed.

"Come on, Katy!" I yelled as I spun around on my heels. It was so unfair. Most people had to try out for things. Justin just waltzed in and people *asked him* to join. It wasn't fair.

Katy's mom picked us up and drove us to the dance studio. I danced so hard that I thought my feet would fall off. But at least Madame Maur paid me one of her rare compliments. I didn't tell her that I was in the school musical, or she would have signed me up for the next three dance recitals right away.

"Guess what?" I shouted to Mom when she came to pick us up. "I got the role of Alicia! I got the lead in the school musical!"

"Congratulations, honey." Mom gave me as close to a hug as she could from her position behind the steering wheel. "But I was proud of you just for trying out."

"And Katy got the part of Clarissa," I added so that Katy wouldn't feel left out of the celebration.

"That's terrific, Katy," my mom said.

After we dropped off Katy at her house, Mom turned to me and ruffled my hair. "I'm so proud of you. You took action and faced your fear," she said.

"The first rehearsal is tomorrow after school," I said as we pulled into our driveway. Her praise made me feel glad that I'd pushed myself to try out.

"Hmm? Oh, that's great, dear." Mom's attention now was turned toward the garage. Her usual parking place was blocked by two bikes laying on their sides. Both bikes had been taken apart. Tim was sitting on the floor with some tools, totally absorbed in working on some bike part. Apparently, he didn't even notice the car approaching.

"You want to get flattened?" I leaned out the window and yelled.

"Oh, Kerri, for heaven's sake. I can park out here," Mom said in her Miss Sunshine voice. We climbed out of the car.

Tim broke away from his bikes for a second and waved. "Hey, look, Kerri, I'm redoing your bike."

I didn't have the faintest idea what he was talking about. I peered down at the tangle of bicycle guts in front of him. "Oh."

"Where's Blake? I told you to watch him while I picked up Kerri," said Mom.

"He's in the bathtub. You know how he loves to take baths. Oh, by the way, Mrs.

Jenkins called. She's got the flu and can't baby-sit Blake tomorrow after school," Tim said.

My mother frowned and ran her hand through her hair.

"Oh, dear. I'm supposed to meet with an important client tomorrow. What will I do? Kerri—" Mom turned The Voice back on me.

"Mom, I just told you that I have my first rehearsal tomorrow," I complained.

"Can't you tell Mr. Reynolds that you'll have to miss just this one rehearsal, but that you'll be at the rest?" she asked. "I'll write you a note. Surely he'll understand."

I had a feeling she was right, but it was the principle of the thing! I felt sorry for Mom, but I wasn't the one who'd decided to bring three stepmonsters into our lives. Suddenly, I felt the whole situation was really unfair.

"That's just great!" I yelled so loudly that Tim dropped his tools. Then I stomped into the house, slamming the garage door as hard as I could. *Boy, did that feel good!*

Six

LITTLE did I know what was in store for us that night. Mom and Gary called it a Family Council meeting.

"We're going to have council meetings every other week," Gary announced as soon as all of us were seated in the family room.

"It's a totally stupid idea," grumbled Justin. "Cut it out, Tim!" he snapped, tossing a pillow in Tim's direction. "You're making noises again."

"Will the Family Council please come to order?" Gary called, looking right at Justin and Tim.

We all sat up a little straighter. Gary has that effect on people. Mom was the first to speak. She stood up and fiddled with the bangle bracelet that she was wearing.

"We decided to have this little meeting in the family room because that's what we are now, a family." She glanced at each of us before she went on. "As a family, we're bound to have differences that need to be worked out. They'll only get worked out if we talk about them."

"Does anyone have anything he or she wishes to talk about and get out in the open? This is the time to do it," Gary encouraged.

We all looked at each other uneasily, but no one spoke. I could hear the grandfather clock ticking loudly in the hallway. *Ticktock, no one will talk,* I chanted to myself. Mom and Gary kept looking at us.

Finally Justin spoke, "Okay, so none of us has a problem. So now what?"

"Can't we talk out our problems instead of hiding them until they explode?" Mom asked softly. Her gaze rested on me, almost pleading.

Another few moments passed in silence.

"Boys?" asked Gary.

"Kerri?" Mom asked softly.

"Okay," I said slowly. "I've got a problem." Everyone waited expectantly. *Ticktock, Kerri will talk.*

"First, I shouldn't have to baby-sit at the last minute, especially when I have other plans. And everyone's using all of my shampoo. There are also globs of green tooth gel in the bathroom sink. It's totally gross," I said.

"I didn't do it!" yelled Blake.

"Easy," Gary interrupted. "The point isn't to blame somebody. We've got to talk about what's wrong so that we can make some changes. Let me see if I understand the problems. Someone is being asked to do something with no forewarning. Someone is using someone else's things and leaving a mess. Tim, do you have any suggestions on how to solve these problems?"

Tim pushed his glasses up on his nose. A slow grin stretched across his face. "Yeah, I do. No one around here needs to be baby-sat anymore. And everyone can just stop brushing their teeth." No one dared to laugh.

"I know what you're getting at," Justin said with a scowl. "We're going to have more rules, like no one can touch Kerri's shampoo or use her sink—or they die."

I threw a pillow at Justin. He caught it and faked serious pain by clutching his shoulder dramatically. He looked so ridiculous that I finally gave into giggles. He started to smile, too. Pretty soon, all of us, even Mom and Gary, were laughing. It seemed to relieve some of the tension.

"No, there aren't going to be more rules, except the rule that there will be no more pillow throwing," Mom sputtered when she could talk.

Somehow things got a little better after that. We all voted on a House Improvement Plan that Gary had proposed. This meant that whoever had a complaint would write it down on a slip of paper. The person making the complaint picked a family member to help solve the problem. Possible solutions were approved or denied by the Joint Executive Committee, consisting of Mom and Gary.

Our improvement plan goes as follows:

Problem: (submitted by Kerri to Mom) Someone expects someone else to baby-sit at the last minute.

Solution: (submitted by Justin, approved by Gary and Mom) Justin will baby-sit Blake tomorrow. The baby-sitting schedule from now on will be worked out ahead of time. A coin will be flipped to decide between Justin and Kerri as needed.

Problem: (submitted by Kerri to Justin) Someone's been using my shampoo.

Solution: (submitted by Justin, approved by Gary and Mom) Each kid will have his/her own bottle of shampoo.

Problem: (submitted by Kerri to Tim) Someone is leaving toothpaste globs in the sink.

Solution: (submitted by Tim, not approved by Gary and Mom) Each kid has his/her own sink to mess up as much as he or she wants. *Amended Solution:* (submitted by Tim, approved by Gary and Mom) Each kid will clean up his/her own globs, or he/she will have bathroom duty for the week.

Anyway, that's how we do Family Council. Later that night, after we'd finished, Mom popped popcorn in the microwave for all of us. And we all watched the last chase scene from the TV show *High Chase.* Everybody seemed happy enough.

But when I went to bed, one thought kept running through my head. *How come I did all the griping at our Family Council meeting? Was I the only one having trouble getting in step with my new stepfamily? Was everyone else perfectly happy?*

* * * * *

"White paint, European cabinets, and a stainless steel sink. We'll get rid of this wood and wallpaper. What do you think?" Mom asked Katy, Justin, and me as we walked through the kitchen door after school a few days later.

"I love it," said Katy, who, like me, didn't

have the faintest idea of what my mom was
talking about.

"What are you talking about?" I asked Mom,
ignoring Katy.

"It's time for a new kitchen. I was thinking
that bare, white walls would go better with
the brown, leather furniture that we have now.
Besides, that wallpaper has been up for ages,"
Mom said thoughtfully. She was flipping idly
through a decorating magazine as she talked.

"But I like the house the way it is," I said.

"Kerri, it's time for a change," Mom said
smoothly. "How was rehearsal?"

"Great," supplied Justin. "Kerri spent the
whole time batting her eyelashes at Morgan
Granger. What a cute couple they make."

"I did not," I said angrily.

Katy came to my rescue. "Justin has
designed his first two sets already. Isn't that
great?" beamed Katy.

I rolled my eyes. Katy's hero worship over
Justin was going too far. I'd have to talk to
her and convince her to stop this weird
behavior.

"See you later. I'm going to play b-ball with
the neighbors," Justin muttered, embar-
rassed by Katy's praise.

"Blake and I are going to the grocery store,"
Mom announced. I had no idea where Tim

was, but it was fine with me. Katy and I each grabbed a diet soda, and we went upstairs. We had the whole house to ourselves to work on our homework in peace.

It was so quiet that we actually finished everything in an hour. In between assignments though, I must've answered at least three phone calls for Justin.

"Does he always get that many calls?" asked Katy dismally.

"Yes, from both guys and girls," I muttered. "I don't know how he does it, but he can *have* Tiffani's crowd if you ask me."

"What does Justin see in her?" Katy asked, shaking her head. She closed her books and stuffed her finished homework into her notebook.

I shrugged. "Now what do you want to do?" I asked Katy. She plopped down on my bed on her back with her legs stretched up against the wall and her toes meeting at the bottom of my Mikhail Baryshnikov poster. She thought awhile before answering.

"Go to the bathroom," she said finally, hopping off the bed and disappearing down the hall. A minute later, she reappeared in my doorway. "Boy, your house has changed," she said.

"What did you expect?" I said with a shrug.

81

"I just haven't been over here much since the stepmonsters moved in." Katy said. "It's just so weird to trip over a train set in your hallway."

"I'll never get used to it. I hate change," I said with a sigh. "Boy, I hope Mom wasn't serious about remodeling the kitchen. It's like she's trying to brush away our old life completely."

"Well, you have to admit, things *are* different. So, is Justin's room at the end of the hall?" Katy asked with that gleam in her eye.

"Yes, why?"

"Nothing. I just want to see it, that's all," Katy said as she disappeared.

I shook my head. Katy is the biggest snoop I've ever known. Sure, she's my best friend, but her snooping has always bugged me. When we were little, she used to talk me into sneaking into her sisters' rooms, and we'd go through their drawers, put on their makeup, and check out their scrapbooks.

I jumped up and followed her down the hall.

"Wow," she breathed when she stood in Justin's room. "He has a lot of neat stuff. Is that his very own color TV? And how'd he get his bike up there?"

"He explained it to me once, but I forget

now what he said. It has something to do with that contraption he made," I said, getting irritated. "Look, Katy, I've been thinking. I think it's weird that you have a crush on my stepbrother. He's a jerk."

"I don't have a crush on him. I just think he's nice. Anyway, I don't see why he bothers you so much," she replied.

He's a creep, that's why, I thought to myself. *You don't see him the way he really is. You just see the act that he puts on at school. After all, he moved into my house with his family and took over. He waltzed into my school and made himself at home. He turned my best friend into a lovesick idiot. And the worst part about all of this is that he seems perfectly content, and he never has any problems. He always seems to get what he wants. I mean, he got a new color TV set! His mom just decides to buy him a TV, and Justin doesn't even want it.* But I didn't say any of this to Katy.

"Hey, what's that?" Katy asked as she focused her eyes on a shoe box sticking out from under Justin's bed. She walked over to the box and picked it up.

"What are you doing?" I asked as if I didn't know what she had in mind.

"Snooping," admitted Katy.

"Look, I know snooping is your favorite thing in the whole world, but we'd better get out of here," I said uneasily. "Our new Home Improvement Plan says that we can't touch each other's stuff without asking."

"Give me a break. There's this great box sticking out from under the bed just asking to be snooped through. Hey, look! Letters," Katy said. "Who's Julie?"

There were at least 10 letters held together with a rubber band. All of them were written on lined notebook paper, and the return address on the envelopes was from Justin's old hometown. Each page was filled with large, loopy handwriting—the kind that I always wished I had. All of the letters were signed, "Your friend, Julie."

"I don't know," I replied to Katy's question.

Katy grew quiet. "Oh, Justin has a girlfriend. He has another one besides Tiffani."

"No, I don't think so," I said as my eyes scanned one of the letters. "Justin told me that Julie used to be his girlfriend. But he said they broke up when he moved here, and—wait a minute."

"What? What?" Katy asked, jumping up to grab the letter from my hand. I pulled it away from her reach and read aloud from the paper.

"She says, 'I'm sorry that you hate your new

school so much and that your stepfamily is driving you crazy. And I'm sorry that your dad's becoming an ogre. Cheer up. Things will get better.' What's she talking about? Gary's not that bad, and Justin *does* like it here. Doesn't he have everybody at our school eating out of his hand?" I asked angrily as I shoved the letters back into the box. "C'mon, let's get out of here," I added.

"Yeah, you're right. We shouldn't be in here," Katy agreed quietly. I could tell she was sorry that she'd started the whole thing. We crept back down the hall and into my room.

Later that evening after Katy had gone home, I knocked on Justin's door. Justin was sprawled on his bed with his headphones on, pretending to read his history book.

"You got a couple of phone calls this afternoon," I said, pulling one earphone away from his ear.

"Yeah? So?" was Justin's reply.

"From some of the most popular kids in the school," I added so he would realize that he should call them back.

"Big deal," he said. "Why are you in awe of them? They're just people."

"And they're not very nice people," I said, flipping back his earphone. "Tiffani Pearlman is especially unfriendly, in case you haven't noticed."

Justin pulled away. "I'm not friends with those guys because they're popular. They're just fun to be with, and there's nothing else to do in this stupid town."

"This is not a stupid town," I defended.

He didn't answer. He just turned the volume up on his stereo.

I walked down the hall shaking my head. Justin sure was strange. He seemed to have everything in the world going for him, but he still acted like a jerk. Oh, well. It wasn't my problem.

Seven

A week later, Katy and I were making our way to the drama room for rehearsal. We were planning to walk through, or block, Act III, all the way to the finale. After that, we wouldn't be allowed to use scripts. We had to know all our lines by heart.

"I'll never memorize my lines," Katy said in despair as we plunked our books on the edge of the stage.

"Never fear—I am here to assist you," assured Michael, walking across the stage to where we sat. He bent low in a sweeping bow.

Katy rolled her eyes at him. "Give it up. You can't even memorize your own lines, let alone help me with mine." But she giggled.

"You're right," Michael said regretfully and disappeared offstage to talk to Mr. Reynolds.

Just then, I noticed Morgan looking our way. He headed toward us. I quickly glanced around, and Tiffani was nowhere in sight.

Urgently, I nudged Katy. "Help me! What should I say to him? You always know what to say."

Katy threw me a grin. "Just be yourself," she whispered.

"Thanks a lot," I whispered back.

"Hi, there," Morgan said as he stopped in front us. He was wearing a dark green sweater that set off his broad shoulders. I drew in my breath sharply.

"Hi," I said a little too casually. "Um, have you memorized your lines yet?"

Morgan shoved his hands in his jeans pockets and gave us one of his incredible smiles. "No, but I've been polishing my dancing since I'll be on stage with such a hotshot dancer. I don't want to be outshone," he said.

I felt weird inside. But I rolled my eyes, turned to Katy, and said in a loud stage whisper, "Well, I hope he's practiced *enough*. I want this muscial to be good!"

"Ouch, you hurt me," Morgan said, dramatically jabbing his sweater with his fist like he'd been stabbed.

"Well, you'd better heal quickly," I said, grabbing wildly at anything that resembled wit. It's hard to be witty when you tend to be shy around a guy. "Mr. Reynolds is blocking our scenes today."

"Luckily, my dancing feet escaped serious injury," Morgan said, his eyes laughing at me.

"You know, I think he likes you," Katy said thoughtfully as we watched him walk over to a group of his buddies. "Give him some encouragement."

"I'd like to, but he spends so much time with Tiffani and her crowd," I said. "Anyway, I've tried to let him know, and all I end up doing is sounding stupid."

"You worry too much. I don't think he's all that interested in Tiffani anymore. He still sits by her at lunch, but he doesn't give her that much attention," said Katy. "Anyway, Mr. Reynolds is giving us the eye. It must be time to get started."

As soon as most of the cast had straggled in, we began blocking our scenes. Most scenes were easy, and Morgan was fun to work with. He joked and kidded around, and I wasn't nervous at all like I usually am during rehearsals. Maybe it was because I stopped thinking only about myself and concentrated on the show—and Morgan.

Before I knew it, we were blocking the last scene. In it, the Ringmaster tries to talk an injured Alicia out of standing upright on a flying, white horse as part of her act. The white horse was actually just a cardboard prop that stood perfectly still.

"All right, Kerri, when you say, 'I will perform tonight, no matter what you say,' I want you to turn your body a little more toward the audience!" yelled Mr. Reynolds from the front row.

"I will perform tonight, no matter what you say," I read from my script, and just then I noticed Justin looking at me from backstage. Tiffani saw Justin, too, and quickly walked up beside him. Morgan turned around and watched them closely. *Was he jealous that Tiffani was flirting with Justin?* That thought distracted me, and the last part of my sentence came out as a squeak.

"Pro-JECT!" Mr. Reynolds boomed to me. "No one in the back of the house will be able to hear you if you squeak. And Morgan, turn around, and pay attention."

I turned away from Justin so that Morgan and I could finish our scene. I tried not to listen to Tiffani's cutesy voice coming up from the wings.

"Whew," Morgan said as we were excused to join the others backstage. "That was a real workout, but you were great. Let's get together sometime and practice our dances."

He gave my hand a little squeeze, and I felt a lightning bolt shoot up my spine. *Maybe he really didn't care about Tiffani. Was he asking me for a date?* I threw him a huge smile and made a beeline for the water fountain. Working under the bright stage lights with a guy you liked was hot work.

"Hey, Sis," came a voice from behind me as I bent over to take a few gulps of the cool spray. "Save some water for the stage crew."

I spun around and came face to face with Justin.

"I'm not your sis," I reminded him, wiping my mouth and starting to walk away. *Why did Justin have to sign up for stage crew and hang around bugging me? Why couldn't he be happy doing something else?*

Justin raised his eyebrows at me. "Did Granger ask you out?"

"It's none of your business," I said. What I really wanted to do was sing out, *Yes,* but I wasn't sure if it *was* a date.

"I'm just trying to show interest, and you bite my head off." Justin kicked at a stack of scripts piled near the wall.

"You're just being nosy," I accused.

"You're always such a snob." Justin shoved his thumbs in his belt loops and walked away.

I can't stand him, I said to myself as I made

my way back to Katy and Ashley. We sat down on a stack of scenery boards to watch Meghan's scenes being blocked. Justin sat on the other side of the stage across from us and sulked.

"Something's bugging Justin," Katy murmured to me. "Oh, yeah, I forgot to tell you. I heard Justin got benched during P.E. today for mouthing off to Coach Fuller. Fuller says he'll get suspended the next time he gets into trouble."

"That sounds like the way Justin's been acting at home," I said thoughtfully. Silently, I wondered if Justin was starting to act crabby at school just like he did at home.

Mr. Reynolds clapped his hands together. "Singers! Singers! Get onstage!"

Since that included us and practically everyone else in the cast, we didn't have any more time to discuss Justin.

After rehearsal was finished for the day, I didn't see Justin around anywhere, so I started walking home alone. Katy's mom picked her up because she had to go to her cousin's house for dinner. That meant that I had to do homework alone today.

Feeling pretty lonely, I went home, yelled "hi" to Mom, and changed into my leotard. I figured I might as well practice some of

Alicia's dance steps for a while before dinner.

As I warmed up, I wondered if Morgan really would call to set a date to practice with me. That thought sent more tingles running through me. My thoughts went over that a few more times, and then I thought about Justin and his getting benched at school today. That had me puzzled. But then again, hadn't those letters that Katy and I snooped through hinted that Justin was having some problems in his new school—and at home?

"Maybe I'm not the only one who's having trouble adjusting to a new family formula," I said slowly to Percy, who was watching me from the windowsill. "Some of us just hide it better than others."

Percy yawned.

I heard a knock on my door just then. "It's Tim," the voice on the other side of the door called.

He walked into my room. "We're playing football on the lawn. Do you want to play?"

"No, I don't think so," I said.

"Aww, come on," Tim persisted.

I guess I was touched that he'd come upstairs to ask me, so I finally gave in. "Oh, all right. But I'm just going to play for a little while," I said and reached for my sneakers.

At least Tim was better than no company. And I could prove to Tim that all girls aren't wimps.

A couple of Tim's new friends were out on the lawn throwing passes. After a while, Mom pulled her car into the driveway. She walked inside and quickly put away the groceries. Then both she and Blake came outside to join in our game.

"Okay," Tim said, as he threw the ball hard at me. My eyes filled with tears as the ball smacked my palm, but I threw it back without missing a beat. My team had advanced a few yards when Gary drove up the driveway. When he saw the game in progress, he tossed off his jacket, set down his briefcase, and came over to play, too.

The game actually was starting to be a lot of fun.

"Hey, here comes Justin!" one of the boys shouted. "Come on. We need a quarterback!"

"No, thanks," Justin said, looking sullen. His hands were shoved in his pockets. I caught him glaring at me.

Well, if he didn't want to be part of the fun, then that was his problem, I thought as I went out for a long pass.

After the game, we all sat down for dinner. Mom had invited all of Tim's friends to stay and eat dinner with us.

"Thanks, Mrs. Freeman!" they cheered.

My head jerked up as they said that. It still was weird for me to hear people call my mom by someone else's name.

I even relaxed after a little while. Dinner was noisy and fun. And I had to admit that if you could ignore Justin, being part of the big, loud Freeman family wasn't all that bad. Still, I'll always be a Rutherford.

Eight

THE next day on the way to school, I asked Justin about his run-in with Coach Fuller.

"Oh, it was nothing really," Justin said with a shrug. "He just keeps getting on my case for everything. The teachers at this school are total pains."

"Oh, like they never told you what to do at your other school?" I asked with a shrug as I adjusted my ballet bag on my shoulder.

Justin dribbled on ahead without answering.

The morning passed by uneventfully. The highlight was when I received a *B+* for an English composition that I'd written about my favorite vacation. I wrote about when Mom and I spent a week together at the beach a couple of years ago. We had so much fun swimming, dancing in the sand, and going to great restaurants together. Those times were

97

special, and I remembered them often now because our lives seemed to have changed so much. *Mom would be happy with that grade,* I thought.

When the bell finally rang for lunch, I realized that I was starved. "Yuck! Plain old fish sticks," I announced to Katy, Meghan, and Ashley as we took our places in the lunch line.

"They *could* be fish sticks," Katy said, peering suspiciously at the fried lumps on our trays. "It looks like fish. Maybe it's some biology specimen. That reminds me, Kerri. Guess what? Justin got moved next to me during science class today."

Just then, I saw Justin out of the corner of my eye approaching our table with Tiffani right behind him. "Don't look now, but here he comes with Tiffani," Ashley whispered.

Justin passed by our table, thumped me on the head with his basketball, and said "hi" to Katy. At that moment, Tiffani grabbed his arm and whispered something in his ear. They both burst into laughter.

Katy's face colored.

"I guess he really does like her," Meghan said, watching them as they went to their table.

"He does not. Isn't Tiffani following *him?*"

I asked, looking at Katy. The trouble was, I really didn't know if that was true or not. But it made me feel sick to my stomach that Katy's feelings were being hurt by Tiffani and my jerk of a stepbrother.

We ate our fish sticks and talked about nothing important until a commotion from the popular table interrupted us. Suddenly, a fish stick covered with ketchup sailed past me. It just missed Meghan and splattered against the lime-green, cafeteria wall.

"Oh, no! It's a food fight!" shouted Katy. We all ducked as bits of food flew over our heads. Above the noisy laughter and shrieks that followed, I heard Tiffani's shrill voice.

"Waaaay to go, Justin!" she squealed.

Had Justin started it? I thought angrily. I felt my stomach twist into knots. Okay, so I wasn't the eighth-grade class goody-goody, but it made me mad that Justin would start throwing food at me and my friends. Just then two french fries splatted against my white blouse, leaving a sticky red mess.

"I'll be right back," I said grimly to the girls at my table, plucking the food off my shirt. With french fries in hand, I marched up to Justin. I wiggled one right in front of his nose. "Look, jerk. You and your not-so-funny friends had better keep your food at your own table, or else—" I began.

But before I could finish my sentence, a strong, tweed-jacketed arm tapped me on the shoulder. I whirled around to see that it was Mr. Richert.

"Young lady," he said, looking at me with gold-rimmed glasses. "What is the meaning of this? Did you start this food fight?"

I heard Tiffani snorting behind me as I stammered to try to say that I hadn't started it. But I stole a look at Justin, and I realized that I couldn't tell Mr. Richert who I thought really had caused the food fight. If Justin got suspended from school, Gary would go crazy. Family loyalties sprang up at the weirdest times.

"You're coming with me," Mr. Richert said sternly.

As I walked ahead of him toward the principal's office with my face flaming, I devised several slow and painful tortures that I'd like to try out on my monstrous stepmonster.

Later, when Katy's mom dropped me off after ballet class, I went into the kitchen to grab something to eat and to tell Mom about my English grade and the awful events of the day. Luckily, Mr. Richert hadn't punished me, and that was probably because until now I'd always been a model student. He had just lectured me, and said that he was disappointed in my behavior.

Boy, was Justin going to get it when I saw him. Maybe I ought to tell Gary. After all, Justin deserved to get into trouble. I toyed with the idea of slipping something into the suggestion box, like *Problem: someone letting someone else take the blame for something he did.*

Well, I'd think about it. I grabbed an orange and saw a note stuck on the refrigerator. It said, *The boys and I are out picking up some Chinese food. Back by 6. Love, Mom*

"Yum, Chinese food," I said aloud and fended off Digger as he made a running leap at me. I put him outside, and then I went up to my room and tossed my books onto my bed. I flipped on my stereo and picked up the phone to call Katy.

Just then, I heard excited barking in the hall, the hissing of a cat, and the sounds of fighting on the staircase.

"Percy!" I shouted, bolting from my room into the hall.

I got out there in time to see Digger chase Percy down the stairs. That was weird. For all his faults, Digger had never actually chased Percy before. Scurrying as fast as I could, I ran down the stairs and saw Percy shoot out the back through the doggie door. He slipped under the fence, but Digger, who was too big, threw himself against the fence barking with frustration. His prey was getting away.

"You stupid dog," I shouted at Digger as I ran past him and threw open the gate to follow Percy. Percy was an indoor cat, and he never went outside. "If he gets hurt, you're dead meat!"

My heart began racing in my chest as I ran down the driveway in hot pursuit of my cat. I searched in the front yard under the rose bushes, but there was no sign of Percy.

"Did you lose something?" Justin asked as he dribbled his basketball up the driveway.

I deliberately ignored him as I crawled through the bushes, whistling and snapping my fingers. "Percy! Percy!" I called. Then I started down the street peering intently into the neighbors' well-kept yards for any sign of my cat.

"What did you lose?" Justin persisted. He was about two steps behind me.

"Percy. Your stupid dog chased him outside, and now I can't find him anywhere. Now are you happy? Can you do anything else to wreck my life?" I yelled.

"No, I'm not glad," said Justin, but in a subdued voice. "Look, Kerri, I want to explain about this afternoon."

"I DON'T HAVE ANYTHING TO SAY TO YOU!" I yelled at him.

"Quit yelling, and listen!" Justin shouted back. I ignored him and continued my search. Justin followed me, and we combed the whole street together in silence.

As I turned toward home, I tried not to let my worried feelings spill over into tears. *Percy will be home when I get home,* I said to myself. He wasn't, but Mom, Gary, and the boys were.

"We got Chinese food," announced Blake, holding up two greasy cartons.

"Mom, Percy's gone," I choked out, not even looking at the food. I spilled out my story about Percy, not sparing any of Digger's role in the whole mess.

"It wasn't Digger's fault. It's an instinct. Dogs chase cats," said Tim angrily.

"He's right," added Justin.

"I've told you boys that dog needs training," Gary said sternly.

He scowled at his sons. "Now let's all calm down, and we'll organize a search party to find him."

"That's a good idea," said my mom brightly. "After all, Percy couldn't have wandered very far."

Just then, the phone rang. Mom got it, and I could see her brow furrow into little, wrinkly lines as she listened. She turned a sharp glance at me, and I felt my worry bubble up into my throat.

"That was Mrs. Beeman," Mom began, as she hung up the phone. She is the lady who lives behind us on the next street. "Kerri, dear," she said as she put her arm gently around my shoulder, "Percy's been hit by a car. Mrs. Beeman says he's hurt pretty badly, but he's still alive. If we rush him to the animal hospital, we might be able to save him."

I was up out of my chair in a flash, out the back door, and in the car before my mom and Gary appeared with the car keys. All three boys were right behind them, and they piled into the car, too. Justin was carrying a box left over from the move and a towel with that stupid *F* embroidered on it.

"For Percy," he said as he slid into the back of the station wagon.

I looked away, burst into tears, and sobbed silently all the way to the Beeman's. I cried even more when I saw poor Percy huddled in a pathetic little ball in a box on the Beeman's kitchen floor. He wasn't bleeding a lot, but his fur was dirty and matted, and he didn't respond when I leaned down to stroke him.

"I just found him lying next to the curb a few minutes ago!" cried Mrs. Beeman as we loaded him into our car.

"Thank you for calling us, Carol," Mom said.

I whispered to Percy all the way to the animal hospital. "Please don't die," I whispered, my cheek close to Percy's shoulder. I wished like crazy that Digger would run away and never come back. I also decided that if anything happened to Percy, I was going to run away from home. I would go far away from the stupid dog and the three loathsome boys who had ruined my peaceful life—and maybe Percy's.

We paced in the waiting room for what seemed like forever until a vet came to take Percy into the back for examination.

"Stay out here, Kerri," Gary said. "I'll look after Percy."

"Don't let them put him to sleep."

"Of course not," soothed Mom. She hugged me tightly as we waited. Then Blake burst into tears, too.

"Is Kerri's kitty going to die?" he asked.

Mom shook her head and turned to hug him. I sobbed harder. Why did Blake care? It wasn't his cat.

"It's a fractured hip," said Gary as he came

back into the room a while later. "Percy's sedated, and he's not hurting right now. The vet thinks he'll need a pin or two, but that he'll be fine. He'll spend the night here for observation, and we'll talk in the morning about the operation."

"Operation? What kind of operation?" I echoed.

Gary explained that the vet thought Percy might need a metal pin put in his hip joint, but that he'd be up and about in no time. As we walked to the car and Gary continued talking, I began to feel a little better. There was something soothing about Gary that I hadn't noticed before. And now we knew exactly what was wrong with Percy. *What was a little operation, anyway?* I asked myself.

"Hey, don't worry, Kerri," Blake said. "If Percy dies, you can get a neat dog like Digger."

"Wouldn't that be great to have two dogs?" Justin chimed in.

"BE QUIET!" roared Gary, glaring at Blake in the rearview mirror.

Nine

FOR the next few days I didn't speak to any of my stepmonsters. I just couldn't have anything to do with someone who wished Percy would die so that he could have another dog.

I couldn't concentrate on school or anything else the day that Percy had his surgery. And I knew I wouldn't feel better until Percy was home safely from the animal hospital.

Gary or Mom must have said something to the boys, because they didn't bug me once during that couple of days. I also noticed that Tim spent about half an hour each evening trying to train Digger to be more obedient.

"It's about time," I muttered as I watched him from the kitchen window, ordering Digger to sit for what seemed like the millionth time. Digger, as usual, had other ideas. I decided that if Digger had been a person, he surely wouldn't have been an honors student.

The day finally arrived for Percy to come home. I fixed up a place by my bed for his cage. The vet insisted that he be protected for a few weeks to keep off his bad hip.

"Percy needs a chance to rest and to let his hip heal," explained Gary as he brought the cage into my room. Tim and Blake filed in quietly behind him.

All of us crouched around the cage and watched Percy. He looked like he was feeling very sorry for himself. His fur was still dull and matted down. He probably didn't feel like licking his fur and grooming himself much these days. "You know, cats are very remarkable creatures," murmured Gary as we sat there. "Dr. Franklin said that they heal themselves in a fraction of the time that it takes a human to heal. They're much more self-reliant than dogs are."

I looked triumphantly at Tim. So much for his thinking that dogs were the greatest things on earth. Tim merely shrugged.

"Can I have a cat, too?" asked Blake suddenly. He gingerly patted the fur on top of Percy's head, but I could tell that he wanted to pick him up just as much as I did. *Well,* I thought, *even if Blake was a pain sometimes, at least he had turned into a cat lover. That definitely counted for something.*

"We'll talk about that later," Gary said. "Let's all go downstairs and catch *High Chase*. Percy needs time to himself."

I got up reluctantly and followed them downstairs. I would have rather practiced my dance sequences from *Circus Town*, but I guessed Gary was right. Percy needed to rest. As we trooped into the family room, I saw Justin sitting in the lounge chair. I turned away just as Digger pushed his nose into my side and nuzzled me.

"Get away from me," I muttered to Digger, giving his nose a push.

Percy might be getting better, but I wasn't ready to forgive Digger just yet. As I sat on the leather sofa in front of the TV, I noticed Mom look up from her decorating books and give me a worried look.

"The workers are starting tomorrow to tear out the kitchen and put in the new one," she said, while thumbing through some pages.

"Great," said Tim. "Anything's got to be better than this kitchen. Those flowers make me sick."

You and your brothers make me sick, I grumbled to myself.

Everything around here was changing. Even the kitchen was changing. Nothing in this house would ever be the same again. Everything was changing to fit the Freemans.

*   *   *   *   *

"He what?" I shrieked at Katy in the cafeteria at lunchtime on Monday of the following week. I had just seated myself at our table when Katy delivered a bomb.

"I told you. I just heard that Morgan broke his leg this past weekend while he was snow skiing with his family at Lake Tahoe." Katy's green eyes were wide, and she was curling a wavy red strand of hair around her index finger.

"Who said that Morgan broke his leg?" I asked, pushing away my tray that was swimming with turkey surprise.

"Oh, everybody's talking about it. He had to be flown by helicopter to the hospital," Katy said. "And he's not going to be able to dance for a few weeks. *Circus Town* opens in just two weeks, you know?"

"You don't need to tell me," I moaned. My thoughts left what Katy was saying, as I pictured Morgan lying somewhere in a hospital bed. *Well, if Morgan wasn't going to be in the musical, then neither was I.*

Ashley and Meghan sat down beside us a

few minutes later and started chattering about Morgan's accident. No one knew anything more than the fact that Morgan was at a hospital near Lake Tahoe and wouldn't be home for a few more days.

Tiffani walked by our table with her cafeteria tray in hand. She was wearing a white skirt and a huge, yellow T-shirt. Her giant earrings bounced around as she threw her ponytail back and fastened her gaze on me.

"Well, Kerri, it looks like the show won't go on after all, will it?" she sneered with a nasty smile. She flung her long ponytail tauntingly behind her as she made her way over to her table.

"What a witch," muttered Meghan as she took a bite of her turkey surprise and made a face. "What does your stepbrother see in her, anyway?"

At that moment, Katy turned to look at me. "Where is Justin today, anyway? I didn't see him in science class."

"What?" I asked. Justin and I had walked to school together this morning. Justin had dribbled his basketball as usual.

"Maybe he was sick and went home," I wondered aloud, although Justin looked far from sick this morning.

"Well, it was strange, because I saw him

talking with Tiffani right before class, and then he didn't show up," Katy went on

"That's odd," I said. Then I whispered to her so none of the others would hear. "I wonder if he cut class."

"I guess he could have," Katy said.

I stored that one in the back of my mind, while we devoted the rest of lunchtime to discussing Morgan and what would happen to *Circus Town* with its leading guy out of commission. By the end of the day, it was rumored that Michael Stewart might take Morgan's place. But when Katy and I saw Michael at his locker later on, he shook his head and flatly denied it.

"I'll never be able to memorize all his lines," he said. "I still don't have all of the lines that are mine for now memorized."

I stopped by Mr. Reynolds' room to see if I could get some answers, but the door was locked.

As Katy and I started for my house, Justin showed up and fell in behind us. "Hey, Justin," said Katy, her eyes getting all sparkly and her walk perking up. "We missed you in science class today."

Justin jerked his head up. "Uh—yeah—I had to go talk to someone about a problem that she got someone else into last week."

What was he talking about? I wondered.

"Hey, Kerri, I heard about Granger's accident," Justin said quickly. Those were the first words that he'd spoken to me in days.

I didn't answer. I just kept walking, swinging my books. I was sure to step on all the cracks in the sidewalk. *Step on a crack, break your brother's back,* I chanted to myself. I knew it was mean, but I couldn't help it. I'd never forgive him for wishing Percy was dead, and for starting that food fight and not confessing to it.

"Aren't you guys going to dance lessons today?" he asked after a few seconds of my obvious silence.

"Nope, Madame Maur canceled lessons this week. She flew to New York to see some ballerina friends of hers," Katy answered. "But you can come practice some dancing with us if you want. Kerri told me that you want to be a rock star, and rock singers have to know how to dance, too."

"No, thanks," said Justin.

"Why not?" badgered Katy. "Afraid we'll outdo you?"

Justin rose to the bait. "Okay, show me some of that stuff."

I glanced at Justin warily. Convincing him seemed too easy. *What was he up to now?*

Katy, of course, was thrilled.

*   *   *   *   *

By later that afternoon I had decided that Justin was a pretty good dancer. I had hung back and let Katy do most of the coaching, since I was still mad at him. Katy was pretty eager to help him out, anyway. Justin was fairly graceful and had good muscle coordination. Katy and I were amazed at how quickly he converted his free-form style to some of the simpler ballet steps.

"Why don't you show him some of the steps that the Ringmaster does with Alicia?" asked Katy laughingly as Justin imitated Katy's arabesque.

"Now don't you get any ideas," said Justin, stopping his dancing abruptly. "I'm needed for the stage crew. Anyway, I'm not so sure I'll be around then."

"What are you talking about?" Katy asked, looking intently at Justin.

Sometimes it made me nuts the way Katy hung onto Justin's every word.

"Oh, nothing," Justin said a bit evasively. "I—uh—have some homework to do." He squeezed Katy's shoulder as he left.

"Oh, I wish he didn't like Tiffani so much,"

said Katy sadly as he left the room.

"Well, if it helps, I noticed she didn't sit with him at lunch the other day," I said, feeling sorry for Katy.

"That could be a good sign," Katy said, cheering up. "And you know something, you ought to send Morgan a get-well card."

I hadn't thought of that. "Yeah, maybe I will."

After Katy went home, I hung out with Percy and tried to ignore the nonstop thumping sounds that were coming from Justin's speakers. Disobeying the vet's orders, I let Percy out of his cage to sit on my bed while I attempted to write another English essay. Blake came in for a while and scratched Percy on his chin, right in his favorite spot. I made him promise not to tell anyone that I had let Percy out of his cage.

"He just seems so lonely that I can't leave him in there all the time," I explained.

"Okay, I won't tell," Blake promised. "Maybe this weekend when we go home I'll ask my mom to get me a kitten. He can be Percy's friend. She always buys stuff when we go there," he bragged.

"Yeah, I noticed," I said absently. It was easy to see that the boys were bringing more and more stuff home each weekend. I also noticed that they were keeping more of it in boxes and dumping it in the garage. It seemed weird to me.

Mom had explained to me one afternoon that sometimes parents who don't have custody of their children feel so guilty that they buy them expensive presents to try to make up for their time apart. She said that they do love their kids, but it's just that they show their love in a weird way.

Blake wandered out of my room, and I turned back to my paper. My mind soon drifted to Justin and his comment this afternoon about someone else getting someone in trouble. Was he referring to the food fight? Suddenly, I remembered Tiffani's high laughter above the food fight commotion. *Had Tiffani started it?*

The more I thought about it, the more it made sense. But why didn't Justin tell anyone? I had almost gotten into big trouble. Luckily, Mr. Richert believed me because of my good record.

When I finished my paper, I put a protesting Percy back into his cage and decided to pay a little visit to Justin. It was time to talk. Walking into his room without knocking, I saw Justin straighten up quickly and kick something under his bed.

"Yeah? What do you want?" he asked, brushing his hair off his forehead in a quick, nervous gesture.

I sat down on the corner of his desk. "Tell me one thing," I demanded, my anger bubbling in my throat. "Did you start that food fight?"

"It's none of your business," he answered.

I said nothing.

"I suppose you're going to spill the beans on me now. 'See, Mommy, what a good little girl I am, and what a bad boy Justin is?' " he squealed.

"Give me a break," I said angrily. "I could have told on you a hundred times by now if I'd wanted to."

"Why didn't you?" Justin asked without looking at me.

"I don't know," was the only answer I could come up with. Just then Blake wandered in with his truck book in his hand.

"Read to me, Kerri. Anita and Dad are helping the men tear up the kitchen. They told me to get out of their way," he pouted.

Blake slipped his hand in mine, and I squeezed it. "I know how you feel," I said sympathetically.

Okay, so I was beginning to get used to the idea of having a stepfamily. But that didn't

mean I had to get along with *everyone* in it.
I looked at Justin pointedly before I allowed
Blake to lead me out of the room to read his
story.

* * * * *

I woke up slowly the next morning. The
sky was gray, and it did nothing to help my
mood. Seeing the construction area that was
once our cozy, country kitchen didn't help
either.

"What's wrong, honey?" my mom asked as
I glumly poured my orange juice and tried not
to get plaster all over my clean sneakers.

"Nothing," I said, smiling too brightly. I
knew Mom had enough on her mind without
my adding to her worries.

"It's the kitchen, isn't it?" she asked. "You
don't like it."

"I just don't like the fact that it's changing," I said.

Mom ruffled my hair, accidentally dislodg-
ing my hair clip, which I straightened out.
"Change is never easy, but it's almost always
for the better," Mom said. "And I'm not just
talking about kitchens. No one ever said it
would be easy," Mom added.

Boy, that was for sure, I thought as I walked

to school. Nothing had been easy since the day the stepmonsters had entered my life. It seemed that nothing had gone particularly right since that day, either. And now something that I'd looked forward to for weeks, the musical, looked like it wasn't going to happen at all!

Then it hit me. Even if Morgan wasn't going to be in the play, I still wanted very much to be in it, anyway. It wasn't for Morgan anymore, but for me. As soon as I got to school, I headed right for Mr. Reynolds' room.

"Come on in, Kerri. I was wondering when you would be paying me a visit," he said.

"Yeah," I responded, settling my books on a desk in the front row. "I guess you know what's on my mind."

Mr. Reynolds frowned and tapped his pencil on his desk distractedly. "I believe I do. I've got to tell you that I honestly don't see much choice. I think we're going to have to cancel the production. I could kick myself for not having signed up understudies, but there are not too many boys here at this school who can dance the way Morgan does."

I swallowed the lump of disappointment that was growing in my throat. I guess I expected Mr. Reynolds to have the answer that would save the musical.

"I'm sorry, Kerri. I know how hard you and the rest of the cast worked on *Circus Town*. I'll make an announcement on the P.A. later today and let everyone know," he said.

"It's not your fault, Mr. Reynolds. And it was fun," I said, trying to be nice as I adjusted my purse over my shoulder. Mr. Reynolds looked as disappointed as I felt.

Katy, Meghan, Ashley, and I met up outside my math class later that morning.

"Hi, Ker. What cute earrings," said Katy. "Where'd you get them? Hey, what's wrong?"

I kicked at the ground with my sneakers. My words came out slowly, mechanically. "Reynolds is canceling the musical. I talked to him this morning. He says he can't think of anyone who can replace Morgan," I said sadly. "He's making the announcement today."

"No way!" said Meghan. "It's too late to cancel it now! The local paper has advertised it. We've all worked so hard. The scenery has already been painted. The costumes have all been sewn."

"We'll just have to give it up and go on," I muttered. "It's history."

"Wait a minute," Katy said slowly as she shifted her books from one hand to the other. "What about Justin? Kerri, you saw how quickly he picked up those steps we taught him yesterday."

"So?" I asked, shaking my head. "Justin would never go for it. He wouldn't do anything that would help me out at this point. Anyway, he seems to have enough on his mind these days."

"He's your brother. Couldn't you talk with him about it?" asked Ashley.

"No, I couldn't," I snapped. "And he's not my brother."

Ten

YOU should have seen the looks my friends gave me when I said that Justin wasn't my brother. The trouble was that none of my friends saw Justin the way he really was. The Justin I knew dropped his Mr. Happy-Go-Lucky face the minute he left school.

Just then, the bell rang, and we all scattered to our classes. I had been sitting upright on the edge of my chair all morning waiting for Mr. Reynolds' announcement. It was like it wouldn't be real until it was officially canceled. But, until it was, I could pretend that somehow the musical would go on.

Right before lunch, the P.A. system crackled to life. Mr. Richert's voice came out loud and not so clear: *"Attention, students! Mr. Reynolds has just announced that due to Morgan Granger's skiing injury, the school musical will be canceled. He thanks all the students who worked so hard on the production."*

I slumped down in my seat. Just like that, the musical was all over. I felt sorry for myself—and for Alicia. The show wouldn't go on after all.

Tiffani Pearlman gave me a 80-megawatt grin as the dismissal bell rang. She ran her hand along my desk, giving me a glimpse of her spectacular nails as she walked past.

"It's too bad that Alicia has to bite the dust," she said, emphasized by that icy smile of hers. "And by the way, tell that brother of yours that he's making a real mistake if he tells anyone about the food fight."

So, it was Tiffani who'd started the fight! "I almost got into a lot of trouble because of you," I blurted out in anger.

Tears sprang to my eyes, but I got up quickly, grabbed my books, and ducked my head so that no one would see I was upset. Rushing out the doorway, I made my way into the school's crowded hall. It was a double whammy to think about the announcement and Justin trying to set things right with me. He really was planning to tell someone that Tiffani, not I, had started the food fight. It was too much to think about.

"Hey, Kerri, tough luck," said someone I

didn't know as I walked down the hall.

Then someone else who sat near me in history class tapped me lightly on the shoulder with a textbook. "Hey, I heard about the musical. That's a drag," he said.

"Yeah," I muttered. Each comment only made me feel worse. Here I'd managed to take action, conquer my fear, and try out for the musical. I'd managed to get through a bunch of rehearsals without throwing up. And having courage had turned out to be for nothing.

I barely managed to make it through the day. By the time school ended, I'd made up my mind to skip ballet class. I just wasn't in any frame of mind to dance.

"You're not coming?" demanded Katy as she met me by our locker after school. "But you never miss class. What will Madame Maur say?"

I shrugged.

"Oh, come on. It's not the end of the world. You didn't want to try out except for Morgan anyway. Dancing will help you feel better about everything."

"I'm just too upset, and I want to go home. Tell Madame Maur I'm sick," I said as I turned around and started for home, leaving Katy to go to ballet by herself.

As I let myself into the house with my key,

I sensed that someone was inside already. I wasn't sure why I thought this since no one should have been home this early. Mom had taken Blake for a 3:00 doctor's appointment. I heard Tim telling Gary and Mom that morning about an after-school computer club meeting today. Gary, of course, wouldn't be home until 6:00. And there was no way Justin could be home yet, because I'd have seen him pass me.

My skin crawled as I heard a faint noise upstairs. I hesitated at the front door, key in hand, unsure whether or not to step inside. I'd always heard that you weren't supposed to go into a house if you suspected an intruder was inside. Where was Digger? Where was Mr. Watchdog U.S.A. when you needed him?

Thinking of Digger made me think of Percy. No way would I leave him trapped in a cage with a burglar or whatever in the house. I tiptoed as silently as possible. I would just get my cat, slip out of the house again, and then go next door to call Gary at his office.

When I got to the top of the stairs, I heard another noise.

"Who's there?" came Justin's voice quickly from his room. He sounded guilty, like he'd been caught at something.

Without answering, I barreled into his room.

What was he doing home already, and what was he up to?

As I flew into his room, I could see Justin quickly stuff a bulging backpack under his bed. Then I noticed that his bike was no longer in its contraption. It was sitting by his door.

"What are you doing?" I asked suspiciously. "I saw you stuff your backpack under your bed."

"It's none of your business," Justin said sulkily.

"Come on, do you think I'm stupid? And don't you dare say yes," I said, marching right into his room.

Justin sat with his arms crossed in front of him and didn't respond. "Are you running away?" I asked flat out.

There was no answer.

"Tiffani implied today that she was the one who started the food fight," I said.

"Look, Kerri. I'm sorry you almost got into trouble about that. I told Tiffani that she ought to go in to Richert and fess up," Justin said in a low voice. "She's even more of a jerk than I thought she was."

"It's about time you figured that out," I said.

"Why do you say that? I was never interested in her. She was just fun to hang around with for a while," Justin said.

Well, that would be good news to Katy, I thought. But I'd have to tell her some other time. Right now I had to figure out something to say—anything—so that I could stall him from running away. My eyes fastened on an expensive, new tennis racquet sitting on his desk.

"I didn't know you played tennis," I said.

"I don't, but Mom thought I needed one," Justin said, shaking his head. "Mom thinks she can buy us, but at least it's better than the way that Dad and your mom and everybody in this town think they can run my life for me."

"What are you talking about?" I asked.

"What do you think I'm talking about, Miss Circus Star?" he snapped. "You wouldn't know what it's like to have real problems."

I stood stunned.

"Look, Kerri, I've got some things on my mind. Things that you wouldn't understand," he said in a softer voice.

He bent over and pulled out his backpack. I stood there watching helplessly.

"Well, for your information, I have problems, too. You probably don't know since you probably weren't at school to hear it, but Mr. Reynolds canceled the musical because of

Morgan," I said, still searching for something that might stall Justin.

"Why do you care? You only tried out so you could get Morgan Granger to notice you. You'll have other chances at him."

"That's not true," I shot back, my face heating up. That had been true at first, but now there were other reasons—reasons a selfish stepmonster like Justin would never understand.

"Couldn't they get anyone to replace him?" Justin asked as he slipped on his backpack and grabbed his bike.

"No," I muttered, my eyes filling with tears. "A couple of us thought of you. Well—oh— never mind. Where are you going?"

"Anywhere, as long as it's away from here," Justin said simply.

"But this is home," I protested, looking around the room that was now totally Justin.

Justin looked darkly at me. "Your home maybe."

"You're crazy!" I cried, my voice rising. "All the guest rooms were turned into your rooms. Your towels with those F's on them are hanging everywhere. I can't take a step without tripping over your stuff and your dog. What do you mean this isn't your home? You and your family have taken over like the hoards of Genghis Khan." I liked the sound of that last line. It had a ring to it. We'd just been discussing Genghis Khan in history.

Justin looked at me icily. Just then, Digger nuzzled under my arm. I stroked him absently, my mind whirling away trying to think of how to stop Justin from making a huge mistake.

"How many times have you said that you're not my sister? So, why do you pretend that you care about me? Just leave me alone," Justin said, throwing up his hands in a gesture that looked like it was designed to ward off the evils of Dracula.

"Okay, fine," I said, after a minute. "Go ahead. But take your stupid dog with you."

"Ker, that's another thing. You have to keep Digger here. He's family now, right?" Justin said in a pleading tone.

"No way. Not that again," I said, getting up and backing away toward the door. "No more family ties stuff. I'm not having any part of that. And—and—oh, you would have made a crummy Ringmaster, anyway!" I yelled just as I stepped outside Justin's door.

"I wouldn't even have considered it!" Justin's voice followed me down the hall. Digger also followed me down the hall.

"No, you'd never do anything for anyone

else in your life no matter what. Oh, Digger, go away!" I thundered. But I should have known better. Digger had never obeyed a command in his life.

I sat in my room with Percy on my lap, and Digger looking at me like I should've tried to stop Justin. I heard the front door open, and I got up in time to see Justin wheel his bike down the front walkway.

I took Percy out of his cage. He flopped on my lap with his sore leg. Digger nuzzled him, and Percy didn't seem to mind.

"I guess you've forgiven him, huh, Percy?" I asked, a little amazed at how forgiving animals can be.

My eyes started to fill with tears. I knew it was no use pretending there were no family ties with my stepfamily. It was time to accept that fact with grace, even if I didn't always like it much. What was it that Mom always said? *You don't have to love your stepfamily, but you have to respect them and learn to live with them.* Okay, fine. I was going to do my family duty. I had to tell someone that Justin had run away.

I put Percy back in his cage, and whistled for Digger to follow me. "Come on, old boy," I said. "We've got family business to attend to."

Eleven

"HE what?" Gary shouted into the phone when I called to tell him Justin had run away. "I'm coming right home."

I waited by the phone hoping that Justin would call and tell me that he was just joking and was on his way home. After a few minutes, I heard the garage door go up and Mom's station wagon pull into the garage. When I ran down to the kitchen, Tim and Blake were helping Mom bring in the groceries.

"Mom," I began, "Justin ran away. I just called Gary. He said he was leaving the office right away."

Mom's eyes grew wide with alarm.

"When did this happen?" she asked.

By the time I went through the whole story, Gary had come home.

"Any word?" Gary asked as he walked into the kitchen.

"No," Mom said, putting her hand calmly

133

on Gary's shoulder. "Let's sort this out first. Maybe he didn't really run away," she said hopefully.

"Mom, he had his backpack and his bike. What more do you need to know?"

"Why did he run away?" Blake asked, biting into a fruit roll that he'd just opened.

Everyone turned toward me. "Well, how am I supposed to know?" I asked. "I just happened to be here when he left, that's all."

"But maybe you know where he went," said Gary, giving me a probing look.

"Well, maybe," I said as I sat down in the kitchen chair. I started twisting a strand of hair around my little finger. "I think he was going home, to Arroyo Grande."

"I might be able to clear this up," Gary said as he reached for the phone that was hanging on the wall next to the bulletin board.

"Hello, Carolyn? This is Gary. Has Justin shown up there? He hasn't?" A little furrow creased Gary's brow. "Well, he just might. He was on his bike. It might take him some time to get there. What? Well, how should I know? Yes, I'll start driving down there. I'll call you if I hear anything."

"Should we call the police?" Mom asked hesitantly after Gary hung up the phone.

"Not just yet," answered Gary.

"Will they arrest Justin?" Blake asked.

"Be quiet, dummy," muttered Tim. Those were the first words he'd spoken since I'd told everyone about Justin's running away. Blake burst into tears, and I put my arms around him and murmured "shhh, shhh" into his ear.

"Now, everyone, let's calm down and—" started Mom.

"—take action," we all said at the same time, and then we all looked around at each other and smiled uneasily.

"I'll start heading down to Arroyo Grande," said Gary. "Does anyone want to come with me?"

"I will," volunteered Blake, wiping his eyes with grubby fists. "I want to see Mom."

I gave Mom a quick look. As usual, no visible signs of Mom's being upset at the mention of Gary's ex-wife. She just finished putting away groceries in the torn-up kitchen as if she hadn't heard a thing. I guessed that even if space creatures invaded the Earth, Mom would cope by carrying on with life as usual.

"Tim and I will drive around the neighborhood and see if we can spot him," Mom exclaimed. "Kerri, maybe you could call up some of the kids he hangs around with at school to see if he changed his mind and went to someone's house instead. I just can't see him taking his bike all the way to Arroyo Grande in the dark."

"Sure," I muttered.

Although my first reaction to Justin's running away was pure panic with a capital *P*, now I was just plain mad. This was practically the worst night of my life, with the musical being canceled and all. And one of my stepmonsters just had to pull a stupid stunt like running away so everyone would worry about *him*. There's no time for *my* little problems. *It just wasn't fair.*

After they had left, I pulled the hall phone into my bedroom and started calling anyone Justin might know. First on the list was Tiffani Pearlman, who eagerly picked up the phone on the first ring. Her disappointment came through loud and clear when she found out that it was only me. But she did brighten up when I asked her if she knew where Justin was.

"What? You don't know where he is?" she asked. I could hear the gossip gears in her head start to turn.

"Well, we figure he's around here somewhere," I said evasively. I didn't want her to know that we thought he had run away. That's not the kind of news you want to blast all over town. "It's just that he was supposed to be home, and my mom—you know how moms worry—was wondering if he went to a friend's house."

"He's not here," she said. "He told me off the other day about that stupid food fight. He wanted me to apologize to you, but I didn't want to."

"Never mind. Thanks," I said as I hung up.

Good, old Tiffani, I thought. I tried a few other numbers, but no one had seen Justin. Finally, when I couldn't think of one more number to call, I hung up the phone. Then I noticed that the house sure was quiet. I hadn't realized how much I'd gotten used to the noise of the boys' stereos, computers, and motorized toys. Now the quiet seemed almost spooky. Feeling lonely and scared, I quickly dialed Katy's number. I really could use my best friend at a time like this.

"Hi, Kerri. What's up?" Katy mumbled in the phone. "I'm eating triple chocolate chip ice cream. Do you want to come over and eat some with me?"

"No, thanks," I said. "Listen, Katy, I feel terrible. I think Justin's run away from home."

"What?" Katy shrieked.

"Don't shout," I said. "I think Justin's run away. Everyone's out looking for him."

"No, he didn't," said Katy very softly.

"What? How do you know?" I demanded.

"I—uh—just know," Katy said even more softly.

"Katy Provender, if you're my friend, you'd better tell me where he is! My family is hysterical."

"For someone who can't stand Justin, you sure are worried," Katy snapped.

"I never said I couldn't stand him," I said. "I just said that he drove me crazy a lot."

Katy softened and laughed.

"TELL ME WHERE HE IS!" I shouted.

"Okay, okay. He didn't run away. He's riding his bike in the Shoe Spot parking lot. I can see him from my window now. He came by and told me he was riding his bike around, and he asked if I wanted to come. But my mom said no," Katy said.

"Thanks, Katy. I've got to go," I said and set down the phone.

Grabbing my pink ski jacket, I dashed out the kitchen door and let it slam behind me. I had a sudden thought and turned around. I ran back inside the house and grabbed Digger and his leash. It already was after 7:30, and I wasn't going out at night alone without protection—even though Digger would probably just lick the attacker to death. *Boy, was*

Justin going to be in trouble when I caught up with him, I thought as I headed down the street.

The more I walked, the madder I got. Everybody was running around looking for him. Gary might even be in Arroyo Grande by now. And I had told practically the whole world that he'd run away. Now I looked like a fool, a liar, or worse!

Digger was thrilled with our nighttime romp. He frisked and pulled against the leash as we turned down the wide road that led to the shopping center behind Katy's house.

"Didn't you learn anything during your obedience lessons with Tim?" I jerked fiercely on Digger's leash. "Heel!" I yelled. To my surprise, Digger snapped to attention and then fell in at my left side.

"There. That's better."

We finally arrived at the shopping center. As Digger and I walked around the building, I spotted Justin. He'd made a ramp out of some boards and packing crates. He was in the midst of flying his bike through the air. Just before he landed, he turned his front wheel to make a loud *whuummmp.* I sucked in my breath and let it out only when I saw that he had landed safely. The parking lot lights somehow made the whole scene eerie.

"Are you trying to kill yourself?" I yelled.

"What are you doing here?" Justin called, riding up and slamming on his brakes right in front of me.

"Very funny," I said.

"What's so funny?" Justin asked.

"You creep. I'll bet you thought it was funny that you had me thinking you'd run away. I told everyone in the world, and your dad and the boys went to Arroyo Grande to look for you. Mom is driving all over town looking for you. I called everyone I knew to see if they knew where you were," I rambled on.

"I never said that I was running away," Justin said, looking at me with steely eyes.

"You never said you weren't. What was I supposed to think? You sneaked home early from school, and you were so secretive about your backpack and where you were going." I glared right back at him.

"So, what *are* you doing here?" I demanded.

Justin's shoulders slumped, and he started playing with the zipper on his jacket. But he didn't say anything.

"I was just practicing some stunts. I came here to get away by myself and think. I decided not to run away after all," he finally said. "Anyway, what are *you* doing here?"

That one stopped me cold. *What was I doing there?* I easily could have asked Katy to come down here and tell Justin to come home. I didn't have an immediate answer. Then, slowly, it came to me.

"I guess it's because I care about you," I said grudgingly.

With my sneakered foot, I kicked at his bike tire. It hurt a lot.

"Yeah, right," said Justin in a disbelieving tone. "No one cares. Gary yells at me all the time. My little brothers are just kids, so they don't understand. My mom is so worried that your mom's going to replace her that she tries to buy us. No one really cares."

"What are you talking about?" I asked. "The whole family's going crazy looking for you. They probably have the entire police force hot on your trail."

"Really?" Justin said, perking up a bit.

"Oh, you like the fact that everyone is scared to death?" I started to yell again. "What's your problem, anyway? You've got everything in the world going for you. You move here and make yourself right at home. Then you make tons of friends with all the popular kids, and you're still not happy. What more do you want?"

Justin leaned on his handlebars and rested

141

his face in his hands for a couple of minutes. He looked like he might cry. That really spooked me. I'd never seen Justin cry.

"You wouldn't understand," he finally said.

"Try me," I shot back in a softer voice.

Justin brushed his face with the back of his hand and then threw me a look that dared me to comment about his crying. "All right," he said.

With that, he leaned over and started scratching Digger behind his ears.

"Okay, so I'm a creep," he started out.

"Okay, so you are," I agreed.

"*You* try to come to a strange town and move into a strange house with a new mom when you already have all of those things in a different place. Try having little brothers that look up to you because you're older and because you're supposed to know everything. You try to move in with a selfish stepsister–"

"Wait a minute!" I shouted. "Me, selfish? I gave up my extra bedroom to you. You get the first shower practically every morning and use up all the hot water."

"You are selfish. You live in your little dancing world, and you cry and pout to make everyone dance to your tune. And whenever I do anything, Dad says, 'Be easy on her. She has had to get used to a lot.' But what about me? What about me and my brothers? Why are we the only ones who have to bend and adjust to everything?"

When I didn't say anything, Justin went on.

"Do you know how weird it is to go almost every weekend to a place that used to be your home? Do you know how weird it is to have a mom who asks you all kinds of stuff about where you live now, how your stepmom dresses, and how she treats your dad? Sure, she buys us lots of stuff, but it feels like she's trying to buy our love. And it hurts."

"Well, why don't you ever talk about your problems, instead of letting everyone think that everything's okay?" I asked.

"I don't know," Justin replied.

"How is anybody going to know that you're upset if you don't talk about it?"

"Everyone just seems so busy with their own problems. They don't seem to have any time for my problems."

"You're nuts," I said.

"Sometimes I think I *am* going nuts."

I still couldn't think of anything to say. So, I just stood there and let myself feel the chill of the evening breeze. I watched the leaves and trash whirl around the edges of the nearly-empty parking lot, and it reminded me of dancing. And that made me think of the

dancing I wouldn't be doing now that the
musical was canceled. I tried to hold back my
tears, but still they came to my eyes.

"I think I'm going nuts, too, sometimes," I
finally said. "I haven't even had a chance to
tell Mom about the musical. She's too busy
worrying about you. Everything's so mixed-
up. But, hey, what do you care?" Big, fat tears
started sliding down my nose.

"So, why are you crying now?" Justin asked
in a tough-guy tone.

"Because I want to, okay?"

"Okay," said Justin.

"Okay, okay," I said and then sniffled.

"Your nose is red," he observed.

"So is yours."

Both of us looked at each other for a long
minute. Then before I knew it, we both were
laughing. It started with big chuckles, and
they turned into belly laughter.

The laughter finally died down, and I wiped
my eyes.

"We'd better go home," I mumbled.
"Everyone's probably going crazy, and I'm
freezing."

"Me, too," Justin agreed. He got off his
bike, and we started the walk.

"So, how come Katy knew where you were
when no one else did?" I asked.

Justin threw me a little grin. "Maybe because I wanted to let her know."

"Do you like her?" I pushed.

"What if I do?" he asked.

I shrugged. "It's no big deal, I guess," I said, even though I did think it was a big deal. And Katy certainly would think so, too.

We walked through the darkness in silence for a while. "Thanks for listening," Justin said.

I shrugged. "You're welcome."

"If I agreed to try to learn Morgan's part in the musical, would you help me?" Justin asked suddenly.

"Why would you do that?" I asked.

"Figure it out," Justin replied, looking steadily at me. "Maybe it's because we're a family."

I stopped walking for a minute and took several deep breaths.

"Maybe," was all I said. I wondered if Justin could hear my heart pounding.

"I guess Dad and your mom are going to kill me when I get home," he said.

"Probably."

Justin reached over and gave my hand a brotherly squeeze. It was kind of protective and nice.

Twelve

THE next day, Justin and I walked eagerly into Mr. Reynolds' room. Within a few minutes of our discussion, the word was out all over school that Justin would take over Morgan's part. *Circus Town was saved!*

The next few days flew by in a frenzy of rehearsals, school, more rehearsals, and finally the dress rehearsal.

"Can you believe that tomorrow is opening night?" Katy asked me as we changed in the girls' restroom after the dress rehearsal. "Are you dying?"

"Nope," I said, hoping she didn't see through my lie.

"You liar," Katy said, giving me a long look. "You're nervous. And you're nervous about how Justin will do. Mr. Reynolds would be upset if Justin blew it."

"You're right," I admitted cheerfully. "But he won't, and I also don't think I'll throw up this time. I think I've changed. Being on stage isn't as scary as it used to be for me."

"Did you know that Justin asked me to the cast party afterward?" Katy asked, her eyes sparkling at the thought.

"I figured," I said. "But, since you are a cast member, did it ever occur to you that you didn't need an invitation?"

Katy gave me a playful shove that sent my sparkly, rhinestone tiara spinning to the ground.

"Hey, you're going to break that," protested Meghan as she picked it up. Her face was a kaleidoscope of color from her stage makeup. She was going to be a great Tatooed Lady.

"Watch the tiara," I said, grinning at Katy. "Anyway, you're lucky that my folks decided that Justin could get out of being grounded that one night and go to the cast party."

"You should have seen Tiffani's face when she found out who I was going with," Katy said.

"I would have loved it. She's not too thrilled with Justin or me for that matter. I'll meet you outside. You guys take too long to undress," I said, gathering up my sparkly, pink costume, my tights, and my soft dancing shoes.

As I stepped backstage, I felt a gust of cool air blast me in the face. It felt good after moving around for almost two hours under hot stage lights. I sat down on a stack of folding chairs and flexed my sore feet.

"You looked pretty up there," came a voice from right behind me.

I turned around to see Morgan hobble up to me on his crutches.

"Thanks. We're all going to miss you tomorrow night," I said. Even though I was sitting down, I could feel my knees get weak as I looked into Morgan's blue eyes.

He came up next to me and leaned against one of his aluminum crutches. The right leg of his jeans was split up to the thigh, and he was wearing a huge cast that was already covered with the wild doodles of his friends.

"I can't say that I totally like someone else being your leading guy," he said, giving me a full dose of his dazzling smile.

"He's my brother," I said, thrilled to my toes that he could be jealous.

"It's really great that Justin saved the musical. But I'm still an honorary cast member, so would you be my date for the cast party?" Morgan asked me, just like that.

I felt my cheeks blaze. "Uh—well—sure," I said. Not exactly a cool reply, but anything that remotely resembles English at a time like that gets at least a couple of points.

"Great. I'll see you tomorrow after the play," Morgan said, smiling at me. "Break a leg. On second thought, don't. It hurt like crazy."

"I won't. I don't think I'd look as good as you do on crutches," I joked. I actually did it! I talked with a boy, joked with him, and lived to tell about it. Better yet, I'd gotten a date!

I watched Morgan limp away, and I sat there for a minute just feeling happy. Then I dashed back to the restroom to let Katy in on the good news.

A little while later, Katy's mom came to pick up Katy, Justin, and me. Justin sat in the front seat of the Provender's car with Katy's mom, while Katy and I scrunched all our stuff in the back with us. Katy's mother was the only one to say much on the way home. I couldn't tell whether we were quiet because of nervousness or excitement.

I closed my eyes and daydreamed about what it would be like to go to the cast party with Morgan. I couldn't wait to get home and tell Mom.

Katy leaned over a huge pile of costumes and whispered to me, "You know, Kerri, I've got to say it. I'm sure glad you got a new stepfamily." Her eyes were shining.

"I guess they can be okay sometimes," I said softly.

* * * * *

The next night, everyone was filled with excitement and anticipation. The curtain would go up in only one hour. Katy, Meghan, Ashley, and I had changed into our costumes already, and we were crowded around the little mirror in the restroom backstage.

"Hand me my makeup bag, will you, Kerri?" asked Meghan.

"You don't need another drop!" Katy said, inspecting her critically.

"Just a touch more mascara," wailed Meghan.

"Oh, no," I chimed in. "Too much mascara makes your eyes look small from the audience. It's an old stage hint for makeup."

"If you say so," Meghan said, still peering at herself in the mirror.

I gave myself one final glance. My eyes were rimmed with black eyeliner. My cheeks were bright with blush. My lips glowed with bright red lipstick. Mentally, I thanked Madame Maur for spending the extra time with Katy and me on our stage makeup techniques over the years, even though mine hadn't been seen until now. I thought that I looked pretty good, if I did say so myself.

"Hey, you guys, quit hogging the mirror," came Tiffani's voice from right behind us.

We all turned around to see Tiffani sail into the restroom in her Beautiful Lady costume. Her blond hair cascaded down against the deep emerald color of her dress.

I couldn't help it. Rivals or not, I had to say to her, "You look wonderful, Tiffani."

Tiffani softened a little under my praise. "Well, you look okay, too, Kerri," she said grudgingly. "Break a leg."

Once we all were outside the restroom, Katy burst into giggles. "The trouble is that Tiffani really hopes you *do* break a leg."

I shook my head, steadying my tiara with my hand and giggling. "Not a chance," I said.

"She sure looks good," Meghan muttered.

I put my arm around her. It was obvious that she was still smarting because Tiffani had gotten the role of the Beautiful Lady.

"You'll probably get the most attention out there. You look outrageous with your tatoos," I said and hugged her carefully so as not to get her wild makeup all over me. Meghan hugged me back.

Katy and Meghan had to walk across the stage to the opposite wing. I watched them go and wondered where Justin was. The stage was still dark, but I could hear the sounds of the people in the audience taking their seats.

"Ready, partner?" asked Justin as he slid up to me and landed a pretend slam dunk on my head.

"Watch the hair," I joked. "It's got a ton of hair spray on it."

"See you in Act I," Justin said, giving me a wink.

I went back to the farthest corner to be alone, warm up my muscles, and make the transition from Kerri Rutherford to Alicia, star of the circus. As I warmed up, I wondered where my family was seated. Even Aunt Sybil had come up from Santa Maria to see the musical.

In no time at all, Mr. Reynolds had assembled the cast and had given us one last pep talk.

"Get out there and give it your best!" he cheered, but I was sure that he was looking right at Justin.

"The heat's on," Justin mumbled looking at me sideways.

"Uh, huh," I said. "But relax. You're a natural."

"Places, everybody!" Mr. Reynolds called.

While the curtain was still down, Justin and I took our places on center stage—the main ring. I already was feeling a bubble of nervousness. I wondered where my mom was sitting. No one seemed to be looking, so I slipped up to the curtain and parted it back just a tiny bit. My eyes scanned the crowd for my mom. Just as I caught sight of her dark hair, I heard Blake's voice ring out over the muffled sounds of the audience.

"That's my sister!" he shouted from the center of the first row. People started laughing. I saw my mom turn around to quiet Blake.

"Drop that curtain!" cried Mr. Reynolds from the wings. I needed no second warning. I dropped it, mortified by Blake's outburst.

"You shouldn't have done that," murmured Justin, coloring just a little. "Brothers," he said and grinned.

"You're telling me," I mumbled. I could feel my face burning with embarrassment and nerves. Why did Blake have to go and yell like that?

But just like that, I forgave him. There were more important things to worry about, like the curtain going up any minute. Already I was sweating. A quick glance at Justin told me that he was sweating it, too.

For a moment, I got such a bubble of nervousness rising to my throat that I thought I might faint.

"Steady, Sis," whispered Justin. He

reached over and dunked me again lightly on the head. The lone spotlight danced off the red sequins of his double-breasted Ringmaster costume.

I smiled to myself. I marveled again that Justin had stepped in at the last minute to save the show, partly because he knew how important it was to me.

Suddenly, the bubble of nervousness popped. I felt the thrill of being on stage and my whole body filled with a sense of well-being. Part of my crazy, new family was out there, ready to cheer us on. And a very important member of my family was right here beside me.

Being part of a new stepfamily might be mixed-up and confusing at times, but there definitely were magical moments as well. This was one of them.

Just then the music from the school orchestra began to swell. And as the lights flashed on and the curtain began to rise, I turned to the Ringmaster and said, "We're in this together, Bro."

About the Author

KARLE DICKERSON is the managing editor of a young women's fashion and beauty magazine based in southern California. She lives with her husband and numerous animals, including a horse, a Welsh pony, three cats, a dog, and two hermit crabs.

"I first decided to be a writer when I was 10 years old and had a poem published in the local paper," she says. "I wrote almost every day in a journal from that day on. I still use some of the growing-up situations I jotted down then for my novel ideas and magazine articles."

Mrs. Dickerson spends her spare time at Stonehouse Farms, a southern California equestrian center she and her husband formed with some friends. She says, "I love to ride my horse around the ranch and people-watch. It seems this is when I come up with some of my best ideas!"